Down With Gargamel!

Luis Othoniel Rosa

Translated by Noel Black

Para Carina
Con mucho amor!
tuyo
Luis Othoniel
Pandemia 2020

ARGOS BOOKS

Originally published as *Caja de fractales*. 1st edition. Argentina: Editorial Entropía, 2017. 2nd edition. Puerto Rico: La Secta de los Perros, 2018

Excerpts from this translation appeared previously in *The Brooklyn Rail* and the anthology *Puerto Rico en mi corazón*.

Copyright © 2017 – Luis Othoniel Rosa
Translation copyright © 2020 – Noel Black
All rights reserved

ISBN: 978-1-938247-34-7

Cover art by Hilary Wiese
Book design by Mårten Wessel

First printing: February 2020

www.argosbooks.org

for Bego and Luis

Capital has managed — like God — to impose the belief in its omnipotence and eternity; we're capable of accepting the end of the world, but no one is capable of imagining the end of capitalism. We've somehow managed to confuse the capitalist system with the solar system. We, like Prometheus, are predisposed to accept the challenge and attack the sun.
Thomas Munk, *Manifiesto sobre el capitalismo tecnológico.*

All creation is a language and nothing but a language, which for some inexplicable reason we can't read outside and can't hear inside. So I say, we have become idiots. Something has happened to our intelligence. My reasoning is this: arrangement of parts of the Brain is a language. We are parts of the Brain; therefore we are language. Why, then, do we not know this? We do not even know what we are, let alone what the outer reality is of which we are parts. The origin of the word "idiot" is the word "private." Each of us has become private, and no longer shares the common thought of the Brain, except at a subliminal level.
Horselover Fat, *Exegesis*

PROLOGUE

In the prelude to *Metamorphosis*, Ovid notes:

I want to speak about bodies changed into new forms. You, gods, since you are the ones who alter these, and all other things, inspire my attempt, and spin out a continuous thread of words, from the world's first origins to my own time

We like that Ovid is anxious to find a *continuous thread* through his book because it's so fragmentary; a continuous thread that will tie all the transformations that connect us to the origins of the universe. We also like the succinct way in which a *thread* emerges even before he invokes the gods: What ties the book together are the *bodies changed into new forms*.

CHAPTER 1
THE YEAR 2028

Wake up, Alice, says Alfred. He caresses her face gently to wake her.

No, let her sleep if she wants, says Trilcinea—defender of the insubordinate, loving Cerberus of Alice Mar's dreams.

A mechanical angel rises in the night and watches. It sees a handful of men walk the darkness, an endless void that touches all four directions, fallow land, abandoned gates and new streams, spontaneous forests and grasslands, every conceivable vine all but swallowing the few bonfires and cook stoves that knit the night from light – clearings that, here and there, wage a losing battle against the forest, superficial cracks where wooden tools have barely scratched the arid soil; from the sky you can see these gaping, vacant pastures deserted for one year, two years, three years, sometimes more, so that the soil recovers its natural fertility – huts made of cinderblock, wood, and tin with solar panels grouped in villages surrounded by barbed wire and gardens; sometimes, inside the enclosure, you can see an outbuilding with a campfire kitchen on the side; villages dispersed in between entire towns in ruins, returned to the foliage; business districts repurposed as fortresses or deserts, the skeletons of the edifices of American companies that abandoned the island as soon as commerce went to shit, streets in ruin, churches at the center of towns—churches more than 200 years old that now serve as shelter; in the plazas, empty for decades, now there are blacksmiths, carpenters, dressmakers, and artisans; endless trails; mountains and valleys of lone-

liness and ruin, until you get to the city, the only place with electricity, overpopulated, with lights that wink from the darkness, that cloak the outskirts; in the suburbs it watches a dozen rich families hidden behind guarded walls, a whole militarized town sealed off from the rest of the population; and beyond: the urban chaos overflowing, accompanied and measured by constant blackouts, rhythm and reminders that this world of petroleum will end, the cough of an organism old before its time barely surviving on a respirator.

The mechanical angel is a drone. And it watches over Puerto Rico in the year 2028. I don't want her to sleep here in the bar, Trilci. She's got enough problems sleeping as it is.

Alice wakes up. She lifts her head up off the table, goes to the bathroom, snorts a line of coke, and comes back ready. She even wants to go dancing. They're in a sort of a semi-decadent hipster bar in Santurce just a few blocks from their place. Alice and Trilci tell Alfred to come dance. Alfred, who just arrived after preparing tomorrow's lectures, doesn't want to. He tries to put on a serious face.

Chicas, I'm a bit out of sorts.

And who *isn't*!? one of them shouts back.

It's not the blackouts, or the lack of food that bother Alfred; he's hearing Smurfs again. Alice and Trilci don't care. Alfred wanted to stay home and read. And Alice, who starts work at a bar just a few blocks from here in a couple of hours, didn't want to go out. Trilci, who goes to work tomorrow at 7:30 a.m., and who has a gringo boyfriend who hates Puerto Rico and prefers to stay home and read, didn't want to go out either. In the end, none of the three wanted to go out. But that's what unites us.

So Alice convinced Trilci to go out because she didn't want to have to fight with Alfred alone. And she knew that Trilci was looking for any excuse to get out of the house. But Trilci, who used to date Alfred, couldn't deal with Alfred's bullshit for more or less the same reason that she — victim of a series of gringo boyfriends — was incapable of putting up with the righteous solitudes of her latest. And so it was that Trilcinea called El Jefe and invited him to hang out, promising him two things: first, that Alfred is in a bad way and needs him (she didn't know this for certain, but figured it was true from Alice's tone of voice); and, second, that Alfred would want to have another of his recording sessions in which, continuing the tradition of his deceased friend O, they would work on a book of conversations about what they called, pretentiously, *Conversations on the Collapse of Modernity*. All three of them had convinced themselves they were blackmailing each other. Not me. I know they just want an excuse to go out drinking during the blackouts.

Alfred opens his mouth again.

They come from little places. For example, I opened the medicine cabinet this morning at 6 a.m. and the voices spilled out.

Alice despairs.

Oh Alfred, I always hear voices in my head at 6 in the morning. Just ignore them..

Trilci, expert in the dynamics of Alfred's relationship with Alice, changes the subject.

Alice, how are you? This change must be strange for you. A whole box of changes — big changes and little changes — but fuck, here you are working in a bar full of drunks on this strange island.

Well, it's fun. And besides, I make more money than Alfred.

Alfred, frustrated, goes to the bathroom to powder his nose and comes back with small, individual baggies for each of the girls. This justifies his pathetic sense of manhood (though he would never utter that word). If he can't be attractive to the woman he loves, and the woman he loved, at least he can provide other substances, be a man of substance, in his way. And the island is overrun with drugs. From the Colombian cocaine, to the heroin that the soldiers brought back from Afghanistan, to the marijuana produced locally, to the pharmaceuticals — all that cargo en route to the United States stayed there without a buyer when the ports closed. In fact, drugs are the only thing in abundance on that panoptical island.

Trilci comes back from the bathroom in the darkness of yet another blackout. She complains that the coke is too strong, that she doesn't like it (she always complains that she doesn't like coke, but of course she finishes half the baggie in one snort), then rolls another blunt.

They talk about the school where Alfred and Trilci work, about poetry, about the stubbornness of Puerto Ricans who keep writing poetry as the island drowns. Alice tells Trilci that she admires how much she reads young writers, that to her it's too much work. She loves the chapbooks the young writers keep putting out on their little DIY presses in spite of the fucking mess of everything, but it's hard for her to read them because there's something she doesn't understand, something that makes her sad.

Literature *for what?* she says to herself more than to Trilcinea.

They talk about what's happening in Bolivia and New York. Alfred wants to talk about the teacher's strike that's about to happen in Santurce. Trilci and Alice say the strike won't work if they close the cafeterias, that the cafeterias have to stay open, that the most important thing about education right now isn't education or the labor conditions of the teachers. The only thing that matters is that the children have enough to eat. Alice says the teachers should become cooks during the strike, and that the school cafeterias should feed everyone. This will win the support of the people. What we need is direct action, not protest. Take all the food that gets lost in the refrigerators during the blackout and serve lunch in the school cafeterias to everyone who's hungry. This would be true civil disobedience.

Trilcinea and Alfred nod enthusiastically.

Alfred hears voices. Alice cooks. Trilcinea smokes weed. These are all ways to keep the horror outside the perimeter — forms of survival, some more admirable than others. Or better: these are ways of *guarding* the perimeter. And this is exactly what Alice says to Alfred, still brooding.

Alfred: Go guard the perimeter.

Like an idiot, he takes her literally. He leaves the bar and walks around the block to make sure everything's alright. Only when he gets back does he realize that he has no idea what "guard the perimeter" means, but that it sounds like something military. *How do you guard the perimeter? Piss on every corner?*

Crying with laughter, Trilci and Alice demand "a report from the perimeter." Alfred tells them that he divided all their remaining money, cigarettes, and lighters among the homeless in the neighborhood. Alice remembers that she could never trust El Jefe or Professor O around the homeless because they'd just give them everything. One time, O came back into a bar without shoes after smoking a cigarette because a drifter he met had convinced him his shoes were bourgeois while El Jefe nodded like an idiot.

Chicas, forgive the interruption, but I really need to tell someone. It's getting worse every day. And right now, while I was just opening this beer, I heard them again — the voices. They're constantly interrupting my life. How can I teach, how can I participate in the protests if I'm going crazy?

Seeing that he needs a distraction, Alice takes a jar of pickled eggplant out of her bag and tells Alfred to trade it for beers while she divides another jar among the other tables because... well, people are hungry. Trilci takes a deep breath. She thinks about her gringo boyfriend back at the house, alone, probably hungry, obstinately reading Plato. Later, while Alice talks to strangers and shares her pickled eggplants, Alfred takes the opportunity to confront Trilci.

I know Alice is sick of me, and sick of the voices, but what's up with you? Don't you care about me anymore? Aren't we still friends?

Blackmail.

Fine. Go ahead. When did you start hearing the Smurfs?

When O died, I guess.

Got it: You're in mourning. You read Freud. Do the work. Problem solved.

C'mon, it's not that simple.

Yes, it is *that* simple. The only thing that isn't simple is that you, in your melancholic's narcissism, abandoned Alice. You brought her to Puerto Rico a year ago after she left everything behind in Brazil to come to this putrid, shit-hole of an island in the middle of the energy crisis. She doesn't know this place, and it's falling apart. You haven't been there for her. The only thing you do is give her drugs and complain about your fucked up head. Look at her, dumbass—she wants to do things, make friends, have a life. And all you do is complain about everything. Alice's jarred foods are going to save the world and your narcissism is killing us.

I knew I could count on you for support... asshole.

After he insults her, Trilcinea passes Alfred the blunt, which he gladly accepts with affectionate silence. What you pickle, what you dry, what you guard beneath the soil so you can eat in the future. Those who preserve something for tomorrow, the salt of the earth, and so on. There's salt in the conversations. Salt to preserve something in the midst of the mayhem.

Another blackout.

And from the darkness, El Jefe, confused, emerges from between the tables, looking for his friends. He melts into a hug with Alfred. He, O, and Alfred studied together at Princeton, but he didn't finish his dissertation, went back to Puerto Rico, and went to teach at a school in Río Piedras. He has the advantage that his parents were doctors and were able to leave him some money. Money that no longer has value in the crisis, but that allowed him, after his parents died, to build a refuge in Isabela called The Cathedral where some of his colleagues and lots of students live. The Cathedral is one of those groups that voluntarily renounce electricity and receive special subsidies and resources from the military to become independent from the state and its economy.

But I'm not running it well, admits El Jefe, frustrated with himself, an almost autistic frustration, as though he were talking to himself, looking not at them, but at the ground. The group is dedicated to disseminating knowledge about practical engineering for all. El Jefe teaches science, math, and was one of the first to warn people to sell their cars before the economy collapsed when gas prices spiked. He's tall, brown, athletic, and, unlike most of his friends, takes care of himself. Trilci and Alice shower him with kisses. Alfred wants to be jealous, but can't.

El Jefe's not interested in keeping the horror at the perimeter. He's fight, not flight. But, though he'd never admit it, he gets bored with his activist friends at The Cathedral. When Alfred accuses him of being overly idealistic, El Jefe's response is always the same:

All I do in these groups is lose my idealism. I go to the endless general assemblies with my *compañeros* to kill my idealism.

Alfred gets pissed every time he says this.

So am I not your *compañero*?

Only with them, his friends, and not with his activist comrades, can El Jefe talk about the things he doesn't understand. And only with them do the things he doesn't understand cease to cause him anxiety. Which is to say that, anxious as he is, he feels relaxed among his crazy friends there in the midst of "the end of modernity."

El Jefe takes a small drag off Trilci's blunt and goes to the bar to trade a few pounds of *yuca* with onions for a bottle of rum. He comes back to the table with the rum and what's left of the *yuca*. Alfred starts to drink as if the world were about to end this very instant. Alice and Trilci are too coked up to eat, and share what's left of the pickled eggplant with the rest of the table.

How are you, Alfred? El Jefe asks — a *How are you?* that actually means something.

The *How are you?* that's pure comfort.

Not so good, Jefe. I think I'm losing it again.

¡*Deixa o cara falar, porra!*

Alice reverts to her native Portuguese when Alfred exasperates her. El Jefe, nevertheless, has more patience with his friend. El Jefe has something of the wide-eyed child at the zoo in him when he talks to his friend.

What is it, brother?

I don't know. It's been days out of orbit, and I'm hearing voices again. I've been writing down the things they tell me in this little notebook. And sometimes they don't even speak so much as suggest images like this one — look:

El Jefe watches Alfred swallow two mysterious pills, which he doesn't bother explaining.

He used to be more discreet, thinks/knows El Jefe.

El Jefe grabs Alfred's notebook and begins to read it with great interest in the light of an oil lamp. He understands, not without patience, that Alfred's craziness is a show — his way of making himself interesting, of conjuring the angel — his way of making literature and living it. He knows that the little notebook is a box in which he's piecing together a novel, or something better...

Don't listen to him, Jefe, seriously! I'm telling you for real that there's no end to it, Alice warns him.

Yeah, don't listen to him, bro, Trilci chimes in.

Fuck all y'all.

But El Jefe also knows that Alfred's stories aren't all fictions. Or, more to the point, that Alfred suffers his fictions, and that his suffering converts those fictions into realities. It strikes him as curious that Alfred calls the voices Smurfs, and that those Smurfs tell him that Gargamel died, and that while he was alive the Smurfs hated him, but, now that he's dead, that they miss him. Despicable dwarves with nostalgia for their oppressor. El Jefe remembered that Professor O always talked about the Polish Smurfs before he died.

Together, Trilci, Alice, Alfred and El Jefe reconstruct O's story about the Polish Smurfs, each one providing key facts — disorganized, pixilated.

It all began in the 80s in Poland. At the time, confronting the communist regime could land you in jail, or worse. Any form of protest required great valor and ingenuity. One particularly clever group was *Pomaranczowa Alternatywa* (Alternative Orange) — half-punks who brought creative absurdity and meaninglessness to political protests. For example, when anti-government graffiti would immediately get covered up with big blobs of white paint, Alternative Orange started painting Smurf stencils on top of the blobs to mock the censorship. Almost overnight, as though they were breeding, the Smurfs appeared on walls all over the city. They became symbols of Polish dissent, and they soon came to life. Hundreds of people dressed up as orange Smurfs began to show up in the streets demanding, among other absurdities, the resignation of Gargamel. In this way, through the use of allegory and metaphor (saying it without *saying it*), they managed to carry out dozens of protests without getting arrested. What self-respecting officer would arrest a Smurf for participating in a plot to overthrow Gargamel? Absurdity circumvented authority.

When they're done reconstructing the story, El Jefe understands the obvious, which Trilci already understood: Alfred misses his friend O, the only one as nuts as him. Friends don't need much to understand one another, and El Jefe brings the conversation full circle:

Alfred, *compa*, it might be time to lay off the drugs.

Nossa!

Trilci and Alice crack up.

Alfred stuffs his mouth full of *yuca* and onions as he nods to El Jefe.

You might be right, but the weed helps with the voices. Besides, it's not the drugs; it's the drinking.

He washes the *yuca* and onions down with another shot of rum (Troglodyte!). Wise as ever, El Jefe changes the subject without changing it, getting to the point.

Do you guys remember that manual that O wrote, *How To Never Be Sober Without Fucking Up Your Life*?

Everyone cracks up again, and Alice remembers how the absent-minded O had tried to email the manual to his friend, "La Chilena", but accidentally sent it to his boss, a Chilean, who was looking for any excuse to fire him from the university. Alfred pisses himself laughing as he remembers all the times O sent emails like that to the wrong person, as though his unconscious had its own secret agenda. And the truth was, O wanted nothing more than to get fired.

And so, in that blanket of hospitality that friends knit when they tell stories about long-lost *compañeros*, Alfred feels comforted. He takes out his old cassette recorder and, there in the socialized darkness of the bar, asks El Jefe to help him organize his thoughts.

Alice and Trilci keep talking about O, about the school cafeterias, about how Alice hasn't heard from her family in Brazil for months, and, in the end, about what, in spite of all the tumult, classifies and orders reality.

El Jefe tells them about a community in Ecuador that's organized by an algorithm. They have a cashless barter economy based on its available resources that's controlled by a software that uses an algorithm to determine the priority of needs for those resources among the community members. Surveys are taken every two days. The software then evaluates the surveys and adjusts the priorities of the resources and jobs. But a strange thing happened, El Jefe tells them. One day, the software approved only two projects. The first (and most absurd) required that the community begin to set aside a small amount of resources so that in 600 years all members of the community could have the right or the option to die in a black hole. The second project (more realistic, but just as insane) was to build a cathedral. The algorithm arrived at these conclusions on its own by evaluating the information that each of the community members had uploaded. It realized that people are fascinated by black holes, that — along with time, matter and light — black holes swallow the curiosity of human beings. The algorithm had also detected an unequivocal religious desire among its users, even though the majority of them would describe themselves as atheists. That quasi-religious desire — the anticipated death in the black hole — would give unity and cohesion to the group. The idea came from physics. Following the theories of Leonard Siskind, one of the proponents of String theory, if you enter a black hole and then immediately turn to look back out just before being torn to pieces and destroyed by the gravitational pull, you would see the most incredible thing in the entire universe. Inside the black hole, the laws of physics break down. Neither time nor light can escape. The very fabric of space-time turns into something for which our minds have no architecture, though we intuit it in the quantum universe of our own atoms. In that moment — that instant, which could also be eternal, just before death — we would see the galaxy without time or space, the totality of the universe, its past, its future, all compressed into the same picture, like an Aleph. The algorithm thinks/knows this. It utilizes the knowledge of physics to which its constituents have access to offer a mystical experience, but described in the atheist values of science.

La Chilena told me about this group. She spent months obsessed with black holes and other diversions of scale in the universe. She devours documentaries about physics that seem to her much more hallucinatory than science fiction. She's become a junkie, Alfred. And not just for documentaries, but also for news about black holes, which is how she found out about this group. It's ridiculous. The interesting thing is that it isn't the algorithm that unites their group, even though it's very effective at managing the community's resources; it's the fascination with the black hole that keeps them together, that stupid dream that in 600 years their descendents will enter into it and turn around to see them, dreaming, from the timelessness of the black hole.

Alice and Trilci drop in and out of the conversation. They hear the whole thing about the community in Ecuador and their algorithm, and think they would have preferred that La Chilena had been there to tell it. She would have told the story with more enthusiasm (and less sarcasm) than El Jefe, and certainly with more (and better!) blunts. We would have thought about that death by black hole as the birth of an angel. If it's going to happen, we would anticipate that those who volunteer to die would be/are watching us right now. We would be/are their past, and they would mourn/are mourning us in tears that will never end/end as they fall from their eyes.

Alfred pretends to be bored. Alice laughs. Trilci makes a

little girl face like she's in love with everything El Jefe says, but, like all of us, her thoughts are elsewhere.

Alice asks Trilci about La Chilena's recent obsession with physics, and Trilci explains the precise circumstances that turned her into a junkie for documentaries about quantum and astrophysics. That the documentaries help with her depression, that they're a kind of therapy, that it makes her feel small, makes her personal problems feel small — small compared to the problems of the galaxies.

And what's all this bullshit about the Cathedral? Alice asks El Jefe.

Who knows? Maybe it comes from whatever it is that makes anarchists idealize medieval cathedrals.

El Jefe always talks about anarchism as though the whole world obviously knows every detail of the anarchist tradition. Alice appreciates that — that El Jefe doesn't try to come up with some mansplaining bullshit, that everything for him is simple, things that anyone could understand. And he begins to talk about cathedrals, but Alfred interrupts him to ask for a light.

I don't have one, but here's some matches.

Alfred thinks the word "matches" is funny. Matches what?

El Jefe remembers a book he read by George Duvy about medieval cathedrals. The idea of the crystal cathedral — the stained-glass windows, the design — would suggest that it was a never-ending project, that we have to keep adding levels to the cathedral, its form being that of toolbox that never ends, and on and on El Jefe goes with his medieval abstractions that drown all of us in mental architectures. Alice, a fanatic for all things medieval, follows him for a while. Trilci looks Alice in the eyes and tells her that whoever invented the sonnet is better than Shakespeare. She says it because Alice is writing sonnets and keeping them secret from Alfred. Only Trilci gets to critique Alice's sonnets.

Ignoring Trilci and Alice, Alfred takes advantage of the situation, grabs a ballpoint pen, makes a drawing, and shows it to El Jefe.

What could this be, Jefe?

An atom, no?

Obviously, but what else?

Pfft! It could be a bunch of things. Where are you going with this, Alfred? It could be a stained glass window in a cathedral, or a temple, a nuclear bomb, two boxers in a boxing ring, a kiss, the movement of sewing, a snowflake, a cornflake, a diamond.

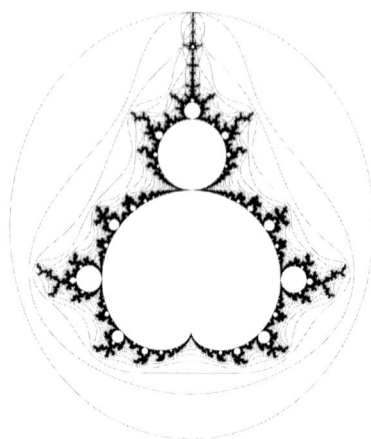

Exactly, Jefe, it could be whatever — a dance floor, a ham, Scooby Doo fleeing a phantom, a medieval symbol for anarchism with the A inside the O; it's DaVinci's man and woman, it's a monarch butterfly — it can be whatever you want. But if you look at it that way, it's nothing — it's an excuse to see whatever you want to see. And if it's nothing, I can't understand what the Smurfs are telling me. How can I understand what the Smurfs are telling me?

El Jefe doesn't know what to say to console him. He knows there's something to Alfred's suffering, but the harder he tries, the less he understands. And in that moment, seeing El Jefe's credulous patience (and she needed it!) with the craziness of their friend, Alice sympathizes with Alfred's desperation.

She knows that Alfred's not made for the coming world (El Jefe knows it, too, and Trilci knows it, but all of them doubt that Alfred knows it).

Alice rubs Alfred's back and tells him it's normal. Take deep breaths. Take it easy. She totally gets what's making him feel this way, that what he's seeing are fractals, that lots of people are seeing fractals these days, that the world reveals its fractals when it mutates, reveals its seams when it's metamorphosing, when it reinvents itself. Alfred stops the tape recorder, then a few seconds later there's another blackout.

And any one of us thinks/knows that only that which mutates provides continuity. And that which is static — fixed — doesn't become, doesn't happen. The static is artifice, fantasy, because there's nothing in the universe that doesn't change.

And with this final blackout their gathering comes to an end for they are no longer so young and must shoulder the burden of the world they inherited and tomorrow there's work. Alice and Trilcinea don't want to leave. Alfred doesn't either, but El Jefe, the youngest, says goodbye and leaves. He walks down Manuel Fernández Juncos Avenue and crosses Ponce de León to Río Piedras. It's a long walk, but he's not alone. There are scores of other walkers — some with candles, others with lanterns — who form groups around conversations, then break up. But all of them pause for long looks at the stars — lost for so long — that have begun to reappear around San Juan after decades of starless skies. Scores of walkers whose footsteps drown out the sound of the cars of a few shameless drivers. Legions. El Jefe walks with the legions of young people at 4 in the morning from Santurce to Río Piedras, full of hopes in a time, on an island, that enters into its slow and foreseeable collapse; legions enjoying the conversation and the long walk.

These legions give him hope. It's a hope inherited, given — an unintended hope that surrounds them, a membrane that imposes itself and vibrates. He sees a hidden light in those walking feet. It's not the Puerto Rico of his childhood. It's better in its way. He knows they'll die, are dying, have died. And yet they walk. We've always known that the dead walk — we who know ourselves to be peripatetic phantoms.

Two weeks later, during the teacher's strike, which takes on national significance due to the popular support for the occupation of the school cafeterias, a handful of terrified police open fire on the crowds. El Jefe rushes in to help carry the injured and gets shot in the back. He dies a few hours later surrounded by strangers who love him nonetheless. In that moment, they love him to the spine, to the entrails, to his final breath, anonymous lovers, like loving the moon or the sun, like loving a book or a good meal, they love the body that dies for having stood with them, without an angel. Alice, Trilci, and Alfred, ashamed and destroyed for not having been there, for not having enough of El Jefe's belief in a new world, come to terms with that disastrous reality of life: friends die.

CHAPTER 2:
THE YEAR 2017

In her first fight for the World Championship, Cristi Martínez, a boxer from Bayamón, is still an apprentice witch. Nevertheless, with every jab she gets closer to her consecration. Jabs that conjure. Hooks that cast spells. She throws a straight right punch as she says "straight." She throws a left hook as she grunts "hook," "upper," and so on. Cristina says these things and they happen. She dances in the ring. Jab, jab, straight, hook, twirl, one-two. Her words punch. When she breathes deeply, she thinks/feels that she absorbs the angel, that it makes her stronger. The angel is in the air. Abracadabra. It's the year 1994 and the public, there to see fights between Tito Trinidad and Mike Tyson, is scandalized by the feminine violence.

"Upper." Her opponent's mouthpiece shoots out. She trained while listening to reggaeton ("Ivy Queen" was her favorite) and salsa because, she said, the rhythm added angel. Obsessive and meticulous, she wasn't unaware of the privileges of her Santeria superstition. Now, in the championship fight, it appears that she's still boxing to the rhythm of reggaeton, with its signature *dembow* beat.

Her left leg doesn't move. It's a column supported by the big toe. She takes a jab to the face that cuts her lip and blood spills down her chest. Her right leg, nevertheless, rotates around the axis of her other leg. It rotates and the angel is back as she dances with her opponent. The key has always been anticipation, and the best way to anticipate the movement of an opponent is to dance. But not now. The angel has acquired a strange connection with her, and she feels it, how it feels. She could anticipate, but the angel says no. But why? Because don't hurry. Because dance a little more. Because don't be afraid to take another punch because that's part of the magic. The public, after all, wants blood. She feels like she's stopped understanding something. She knows that a double left jab is coming. But she doesn't know that, behind the double jab, a right cross is coming, too. She doesn't know it, and she doesn't intuit it. She should duck her head like she's practiced since she was a girl, moving her head under the rope. But she doesn't. The angel tells her no. She takes two jabs to the nose and just as the right cross is coming toward her she understands everything. She understands why the angel's magic told her not to move. Everything moves slowly. Everything slows down. But not her. Her velocity? Fast. She unleashes her left uppercut without thinking. She barely hits her opponent. She takes the right cross but absorbs it. Now her opponent is weak. Feeble while she lifts her chin. And then Cristina Martínez throws her right cross.

Slow.

Every muscle tensed.

Slow.

She wants everything to stay right there. Because her opponent's right cross leaves her doubled over, the trajectory of the overhand right that follows lands like a missile to the jaw. She used her opponent's blow to position herself at the perfect angle — something no trainer ever taught her. When you're at the top of your sport you play by different rules. Cristi Martínez perceives her own joy as she lands this improvised punch — a punch conjured by a counter-intuitive magic that arrives at the always-vulnerable chin of her opponent before the invincible angel. And life. The good and the bad. It all ends with a punch she never practiced.

She's no longer an apprentice witch. She's a world champion. The lights and the cameras go off in syncopation with her screams. And the public, oh, the public, which didn't even know that two women would fight for the world championship before the Tito Trinidad fight, roar, clamor, recognize the glory of the woman dressed in pink, covered in blood.

Tyson and Tito's promoter offers her a good contract. Together with her trainer/spouse, they start selling her in interviews and sports magazines as the most "feminine" and "sexy" athlete in the world. They force her to use homophobic epithets against her opponents. And her husband always threatens her — *I'll kill you if I catch you fucking around with a woman.*

The angel, nevertheless, consumes her efforts, exhausts her body. At 29 years old, Cristi Martínez is made of angel. She breathes it, does it, is it.

And then she isn't.

A tear on the ligament of her knee pushes the angel away a little. Not completely. She's still intelligent. She knows how to cut off the ring. She's mastered the art of doing more with less. Her crosses aren't as heavy as they once were. Her jab is slower. Her legs don't dance now. But now she's more accurate. She works the angles. And she doesn't lose the angel altogether. She reformulates it.

When an athlete intuits the end, before the body breaks down, there's a kind of rejunevenation, light magic of the moment before the weight of reality imposes itself on the aching body forever. She studies the sport. She's not the world champion anymore. But she's got a modest fan base — those boxing freaks who enjoy knowing her, and aren't hung up on her gender. Her love of the sport — the love that brought her to study boxing in the first place — won't wear down as fast as her knees, she thinks.

You have to be hard if you're going to dedicate yourself to this brutal sport in a macho world that doesn't bestow a drop of glory on female boxers. The boy who starts training at a boxing gym in Puerto Rico dreams of the glory (and the pay days) of Wilfredo Gómez, or of Miguel Cotto, or of Tito Trinidad. At best, his chances of achieving that glory are miniscule and risky. For the girls, it's not only that they didn't have a popular female boxing hero to look up to when they started (because there weren't any), but they also had to fight the social stigma of being a female fighter, which was almost as bad in Puerto Rico as being a whore.

Cristi Martínez figured it out early: You have to invent an angel. And you have to meet that angel every time you step into the ring to validate all your efforts and cancel out the stares.

She remembers a time when it wasn't like this, when she was a teenager in Bayamón, and she had a girlfriend that played basketball with her, and for those few months she didn't go to the gym even once, until one day that girlfriend moved to the United States, and she felt so lonely..., and she went running back to the gym to look for her angel, to redouble her efforts, and a few years later her trainer proposed to her and she accepted without thinking because it would allow her to live and breathe boxing 24/7, because she didn't want anything to distract her from her angel, because she wanted to give the girls who might come after her — confused, and looking for refuge from the world in a boxing gym — a hope she never had: glory.

At 32, Cristi Martínez begins to lose her magic forever. Her home is a Hell, and it becomes more violent, more brutal. She fills it with self-hatred, and her angel abandons her. She doesn't want to fight anymore. The ring is cruel to boxers who've lost their will to fight. She takes a couple beatings. She gets drunk. In the press, the same writers who celebrated her improbable rise to glory now use her as a cautionary tale: progressives who once held her up as a feminist icon now point to her as an example of the cruelty of an inhumane sport. Conservatives accuse her of being a lesbian, which is proof that boxing is a man's sport. For three years, she does nothing but line after line of coke.

But all stories — even the saddest — carry the seeds of rebirth. These are the years when Facebook emerges. And it's through Facebook that she reconnects with the old girlfriend from her high school basketball team. She finds a light that has nothing to do with the angel of boxing. She wants to do other things again. In her secret cell phone conversations, in her chats on Facebook, and in her escapes for coffee behind her husband's back, her body begins to heal. She sleeps better. Her joints and her ligaments heal. The pain becomes tolerable. And then one day she fakes an injury because she doesn't want to train anymore. Now without her angel, and almost broke, she tells her husband that she's going to an addiction recovery center in the Dominican Republic.

She runs away with her girlfriend for the first three weeks of peace in her entire life — three weeks in which she experiments intensely for the first time with the gears of love without the mechanics of death.

When she gets back to Puerto Rico she decides to leave her husband. The world has changed. Enough so that she's no longer afraid to come out. She starts to gather her things after telling her husband/trainer who says nothing, leaves, then returns home with a knife in his hand. Cristi is ready to fight and manages to break his nose, but gets stabbed three times in the side. One of the stabs punctures her lung. As she bleeds to death on the floor, he kicks her and screams, *You disgusting bitch, I told you I'd kill you.* He finds his gun and shoots her in the back, leaves her for dead, then gets in the shower to wash off the blood. Meanwhile, Cristi drags herself to the door, and then to the middle of the street in hopes that someone compassionate will help her, all the while repeating the name of her lover as though to conjure her, as though she might swoop down to save her.

A car passes and sees her dying, covered in blood, but doesn't stop.

And then a face appears, but it isn't her lover; it's her angel.

And another car passes without stopping.

And the face of her lover never appears. Only her angel.

And then another car.

That goddamned angel from the glorious night when she became a witch.

And another car passes.

That night when she danced with her opponent to the rhythm of "Ivy Queen," anticipating all her moves. That night when the angel did everything, breathed in her, was her, is her.

And all the cars in the world pass without stopping that afternoon in the year 2017.

Her death has been largely ignored by the press. This morning, however, when I open the paper, for some reason I turn to the obituaries and come across one that grabs my attention:

Yesterday, surrounded by silence and crowned with a wreath of ghosts, Cristina "El Demonio Rosita" Martínez, the greatest Puerto Rican fighter of all time, passed from the world. Her family does not remember her because she had no family. Her country will not honor her because she has no country. Only she — your lover — and I remember you,

Your Angel,
A.M.

Ever since I read that obituary I can't get it out of my head. Those initials "A.M." must stand for Alice Mar. In the months following the death of Crtistina Martínez, I've encountered more obituaries signed "A.M." Initially they were only obituaries for boxers: Héctor "El Macho" Camacho, Edwin "El Inca Valero," Arturo Gatti, Vernon Forest. But then they began to appear beneath the obituaries of forgotten terrorists. Finally, the obituaries by A.M. grew to include the violent deaths of Blacks and Latinos assassinated by the police. 43 obituaries for the Normalistas de Ayotzinapa — the 43 student-teachers disappeared in Guerrero in 2014. There was a beautifully written obituary for María Elena "Lulú" Fernández, the choir director from the University of Puerto Rico whose crackhead grandson murdered her with a machete to the head. All of the obituaries were signed by "Your Angel, A.M."

Alice never admitted to writing those obituaries, nor did she deny it. She and I were lovers by chance and, later, by destiny — distant readers of each others' work. Alice beneath a ceiling fan in a half-restored building in Villa Madalena in Sao Paulo; me in a New York City sublet (later in North Carolina, then Buenos Aires, then Hartford, and now in the mountains of Colorado). And then we recognized each other at a crossroads. To this day I still believe that what brought us together was the need to complete each others' stories, to always be listening for those conversations that cover a stretch of sidewalk in any city. From the mere mention of the words "Tell me" comes our long distance love grounded in words, their nooks and crannies. Those two words, "Tell me", prepare the ground for an uninterrupted continuity, the improbable desire and certainty that the stories will carry on in one another, and always in keeping with the universal law of preservation of information by which everything that happens, even thoughts, leave clues to their existence in reality forever.

It's for this reason, dear reader, that it's necessary to clarify the following: Alice only exists in my mind. She began talking to me while I wrote my first novel. We told each other stories as

I drove around. Later, when they took away my driver's license after an accident, we began to tell each other stories while I walked, while I waited for my drug dealer (they always make you wait), while I waited in line at the post office, pretty much everywhere. She told me stories that I later told to my friends. I can't remember when I actually started saying her name, as though she were real. But from then on, I'd say, Alice had told me this, or Alice told me that. And whether they took pity, or were just humoring me, they grew accustomed to Alice, and always knew when a story was mine or hers. They always knew she didn't exist, that she was an extension of my imagination, a kind of therapy.

Then the obituaries signed by A.M., Alice Mar, angel of the morning, began to show up. It's then that I suspect that Alice, my "therapy," who arrived as a way to maintain my sanity, may have slipped through my fingers.

II.

Professor O doesn't live in the mountains of Colorado. He lives at his desk — appendage and portal — the one constant in his constant changes of address. On the Internet he rediscovers the public square and throws his head down the cyber-hole. He makes long-lasting friendships through sharing news and links, but also confessions. Worlds form in the exchange of information and knowledge, but also in the exchange of emotions that satiate that need for intimacy with people who seem like people you know, but different — close friends you know to the core of their souls even though you've never seen or hugged them. Of course, there are also the flesh-and-blood friends with their equally nomadic paths. And the internet, with its constantly evolving technological communication prosthetics allows you to communicate with them and see them and encounter them arbitrarily in the virtual hole via Skype, Facebook, email, etc., is a necessity for maintaining friendships. But as the years pass, though the friendships don't stop intensifying, they become more and more naturalized in that virtual place.

Every time I travel to see them in person, he thinks/knows, the virtual exchange feels more natural than the physical.

Professor O doesn't just live in the virtual world. He also lives in a world of planes — interminable flights, the cost of gasoline, another kind of smoke that, for better or worse, defines him. And how, you ask, does he pay for all these flights? It cannot be denied, says Professor O to himself, that the university is a place of refuge, and it cannot be accepted that the university is a place of enlightenment. In the face of these conditions one can only sneak into the university and steal what one can. To abuse its hospitality, to spite its mission, to join its refugee colony, its gypsy encampment, to be in the university but not of it — this is the path of the subversive intellectual in the modern university; this is the way in which Professor O justifies his self-image as a subversive intellectual. He steals everything he can from it. He steals scholarships, research funds, travel funds, and every resource he can find and channels it to poet friends who are hungry, to women who've spent years living out of backpacks to make documentaries about Bolivian feminists. He steals books, makes PDFs of everything he finds in the rare books collections and puts them out on the web for free. He steals paper, paint, poster board for protest signs, scissors, staplers, pens, toilet paper, desk chairs, furniture, coffee, food, wine. He steals a lot of wine. Also, one has to incite violence. He instills his visceral disgust for the university and its campus and its cynical, trogolodyte administrators in his students and his colleagues. Without fear, he talks to everyone he can about how much he hates the university. He practices his rhetoric, his shit-stirring campaigns. Some of his students will leave his classes hating their parents and giving a fuck about the 70,000 dollars they spend on a single year of their elitist, white supremacist private education. Steal from academia, sow hate, spit on all of it as much as he can, and be ready to run when they come knocking.

What O doesn't say is that the higher-ups at his corporate private university are big fans of his subversive intellectual act. They laugh at his tantrums and give him the platform on which to have them. They invite him to speak, to expound with critical ferocity, and to excoriate academia and the corporatization of the world. For as long as someone like him speaks from inside their institutions, they can keep swindling millions of American students. Professor O legitimizes that caste of university administrators. While he steals pens, in other words, they steal billions and effectively deny the majority of the population an education while turning them into debt slaves. Close the windows, put up a fence, build a wall around the university, and there amidst the stench of that bubble, Profesor O tries to see the world outside the way a prisoner tries to see it through a keyhole.

Forced to change jobs every couple of years, he roams the silent parking lot that is the United States, and in each of these places he finds the freaks, or those who've lost something, or those who've been fucked over, or those more-or-less domesticated monsters that run their mouths and howl and aren't afraid of being different, the displaced from faraway places who landed there because, by chance or luck (good or bad), they found books in their adolescence and can't manage to assimilate, even if they wanted to; those who manage to have a little life, if reluctantly, and complain, and still manage to enjoy this vast personality desert in which everything is equal and the same, that get bored with the shitty sameness, that spit on the floor and chain-smoke cigarettes and fall in love with things that no one else cares about; that begin with the premise that the world is a dump and they know themselves to be trash, without tears or trauma, and since one is trash, they rummage through it to see what they find without the need to hoard or be important, but only for curiosity, without having children to inherit the shitworld, they share their garbage and curiosity, and stave off their loneliness, and feel good about their difference, in their persistent need to make a difference, whatever difference that may be, green hair, tattoos, transgender, confused anarchists, non-conforming Marxists, poet punks, conservative lesbians, Muslim feminists, crazy white santeras who pray in the name of a Queer Christ, jaded prophets of a religion without followers — it doesn't matter because it's in the difference that we feel less alone with ourselves.

I lived on these meta-conversations with my nomadic friends. Even when we were sober, they became drafts for something to come. Later, they moved somewhere else, or I moved somewhere else, and I'd find myself alone again, talking only to Alice. In my conversations with Alice at night after work we'd tell each other stories about people's lives. Which is to say, we'd summarize a strange or interesting life in an anecdote. Like the story of the life of Amy Bishop who had a PhD in biology from Harvard. She was practically a genius, and got a job as a professor at the University of Alabama. But since she was a woman, her bosses discounted her work even though she'd managed to secure millions of dollars in grants for the university. And how, after five years of working twice as much and twice as hard as her male colleagues, she arrives at her tenure meeting and they're very sorry but they've turned her down. She takes a deep breath, begs their pardon and asks them to wait a moment while she looks for something in her office. She comes back with a 9mm and kills them all. Alice says that these stories we tell each other have an angel because they distill a complicated social reality into an anecdote about an individual. It was never entirely clear to me what she meant by "had an angel." The problem is that I don't remember having written any of those obituaries signed by A.M. I know that we told each other those stories, but I also know that I never wrote them. So, Alice must be writing them without me knowing, and that's troubling, because it means my schizophrenia is out of control.

III

Alice tells me that there are clandestine machines creating other worlds inside this world. That this shit all around us is a shell. When it breaks, the underground work — the work of a few tireless engineers — will appear.

But how will we find them?

You don't find them, O, they'll find you when they need you. The thing is: If they reveal themselves now then it'll fuck them up, and if they have to run some propaganda campaign to convince everyone about their beliefs, it'll fuck everything up. They're building forms in small groups. You have to undo yourself from the angel.

Enough with the fucking angel already. What do you mean by that, Alice? Who is this angel?

On this day, Professor O finds a rare book made of white cardboard that someone slid beneath the door of his office. The cover has nothing but a circle that seems to have been drawn by hand and then digitized and printed on the front. The title is *La dignidad* and there's no author. There's no information about the publication date, the press, the printing, or the city where it was published. Professor O doesn't pay it much mind until he goes on the internet and sees that hundreds of people received versions of the same book in different languages. Not copies, versions. Because when they begin to compare the contents they discover that each one has been personalized. The books have the same cover and the same title, but its contents are different depending on which reader receives it. When we begin to compare them, we arrive at the conclusion that the different versions of La dignidad all share a single structure: the first part is a long list of obituaries of the recently dead, of people who died or were assassinated for reasons of structural violence; the second part is a list of very brief manifestoes that postulate models of social organization in which those deaths would not have happened; and, finally, there's a list of reviews of concrete modes of insurrection that are happening around the globe and how to support them. These three parts are preceded by a kind of prologue — also titled La dignidad — that, without explicitly referring to any of them, invokes classical anti-capitalist doctrines that argue against the alienation of the modern world.

Curious, I carefully examine the book and find, among the obituaries, three or four obituaries by Alice that I hadn't seen. Like the others, they were mostly about people with whom I was more-or-less acquainted such as Antonio Calvo, professor at Princeton who, after 10 years of teaching there from morning to night, the university decided to fire him and Immigration demanded his immediate deportation. Forced to abandon his life and his career — everything he'd poured his heart and soul into for more than a decade — he killed himself.

When he turns the page, O finds a loose piece of paper with a typewritten message inviting him to "write" the book, and giving him precise instructions on how to access an encrypted web page with access to a whole trove of obituaries, manifestoes, and methods of insurrection.

The overly secretive process infects Professor O with a mild paranoia. First, he had to download Tor software that would allow him to use a secure IP address that would keep his computer from being tracked. Then he had to open an email account under a URL that ended in .onion and send a message to another email address with the answer to a very personal question from the loose sheet of paper he'd found in the book. Then he receives a message at that email address giving him an address on the deep web. To access that page he has to enter a password specifically written for him, which he could find on page 55 in that particular version of *La dignidad* that he'd received. The whole process was completely unnecessary, he thought/knew.

La dignidad, or at the least the version I received, doesn't have a single piece information that's not available on the web. The insurrections that it outlines and invites us to support aren't armed insurrections, and the manifestoes, though they're certainly radical, copy versions and variations of the same anarchist principles already commonly known. And so: Why the paranoia?

When he finally gets access to the page he discovers an enormous database with thousands of obituaries listed chronologically, hundreds of short manifestos, and blueprints for specific insurrections around the world. Scrolling through the pages of lists he can identify posts in at least 14 different languages. And when he refreshes the page he discovers the lists keep growing at an exponential rate thanks to curious people like him infected with the same paranoia who've arrived there by following the same instructions. It's a kind of virtual Babel in which anyone can add their dead, submit their own manifestoes, and outline whatever one understands to be a mode of insurrection (though what exactly was meant by "insurrection," Professor O discovers, had lost its specificity on that web page, since just about anything could be viewed as an insurrection up to and including a sleeping cat, according to one group of "revolutionaries").

There is also a template on the page that I could download. Anyone could use that form to create their own version of the book with their own selections from the growing list of obituaries, manifestoes, and insurrections there on the web page plus one's own additions. It appears that there are only three hard-and-fast rules: the first is that you can't print two copies of the same version of the book; the second is that each version must have exactly 100 pages; and the third is that is that the person who receives a version *La dignidad* can't know who made that version. In that way, it's a living book that always changes and updates with each version. It has neither authors, nor edition numbers, nor a press, nor a single language, yet it remains the same book with only minor variations depending on who makes it.

O wants to play, too. He downloads the template and starts putting together a version of the book for his sister, a professor who specializes in 16th-Century clandestine Moorish cultures of Spain. The wife of an engineer, she's grieving the recent death of her 5-year-old, 140-pound bullmastiff, Actaeon, who was the loyal and vigilant guardian of her dreams. He chooses the obituaries, manifestoes, and insurrections carefully. From the French, he translates the obituary of a young fruit vendor Mohammed Bouazizi and the insurrection that followed his self-immolation. He also writes a couple of his own obituaries, including one for her dog, Actaeon, which he places just after a manifesto against the genetic manipulation of pets. Then, using a fake address so she won't know it's him, he mails her the book.

And, just like O, thousands of people around the world do the same. *La dignidad* goes viral. It makes the news and, barely a week later — when China, Saudi Arabia and, finally, the United States prohibit the distribution and possession of *La dignidad* — it becomes a political symbol of something we don't quite understand. And that's when we begin to see the poorly drawn circle on the cover show up in the streets all over the world from Asia to Latin America.

Professor O then understands the secrecy around the book,

and why the web page — full of paranoid obstacles — had to be so difficult to access. In the end, the contents of the book are of little importance: some kind of anarchist tool box or blank canvas. The important thing is the anonymous means of distribution. The book, from the beginning, appeared *as though* it were terrorist propaganda, *as though* it contained the secret of a revolutionary insurgency against the deaths caused by capitalism, deaths of people close to the reader with whom the reader can identify because someone who knows you prepared the book exclusively for you. By acting as though it were something that in reality it isn't (there's nothing in those databases that isn't public knowledge) its prefabricated paranoia infects the global centers of power. The centers of power now feel just as watched as the people.

That night, O goes to bed happy and excited, and he dreams of an elf with pointy ears that moves slowly and tells him the following:

It's not trtrtrtrtrue that there's nothing ououououtside cacacacapitalism. Only the anthroponarcissist humans say that. And the galaxies? The bottom of the sea? Spacetime? The future? The 50 million years of homo sasasasasapiens? The evolution that brought us here, which will cause us to die outtttttttttt? Those who believe there's nothing outside capitalism don't just say it for the sake of conformist convenience, but because they have a puerile ide'a of the world, and haven't realized the terrible interconnection to a long and imemmemmmemmense collectivism, that we've barely begun to understand how young we are, like the monononononarch butterflies.

But if I didn't say anything about capitalism, O replies to the elf, what happened? Did you swallow a Zarathustra?
No. I'm Enheduana, Enheduaaaaaaaaaanna.
Professor O wakes up that morning thinking about me —

his Alice Mar — and wondering how the fuck my obituaries got into the secret databases of *La dignidad* before he discovered them.

IV

Wolves have arrived in the mountains of Colorado. O comes across a wolf den that has the form/leaves the emptiness of extracted roots. He remembers how the *yuca* roots and their tendrils look like angels when you pull them from the ground. Alfred and I had told him about it. And how the negative space left by the pulled root looks like a wolf den. The orchid is an organ of the butterfly, but it's also a mother. There's a genetic connection between them, O remembers Trilcinea telling him. The rats move like squash vines, he remembers El Jefe telling him. Rats are just squash vines, O thinks/knows. Biology falsifies nature to classify it. If we think only in terms of movement, then the only difference between rats and squash is their opposing velocities: one moves fast, the other moves slow. O doesn't know what'll happen with *La dignidad*, but he has visions of the future; of a world of pirates that return to an empty home; of a world that turns night into day; of a fast, easy, anesthetized change. And he sees the world full of umbrellas that reflect sunlight, that float across a planet that looks like another, not ours. The whole world thinks the end of capitalism will be violent, thinks O, but maybe it'll be calm, obvious, easy, without angels, with umbrellas (and we begin to see how, when we say "know," we refer to things that Professor O pulled out of his ass in a pinch). He knows because while he "runs" through the mountains he sees an orchid and a butterfly, and he knows himself to be as much animal as vegetable.

The effects of the sativa continue, but the second dose of kratom has just barely begun to kick in with the warmth of the midday sun. Today is a good Sunday, O thinks. And the sun begins to toast his face. He takes a break at a little brook, drinks some water, walks slowly, explores, and takes out a baggie full of mushrooms that La Chilena sent him. He eats them, and he knows that he'll start to feel the effects in an hour, and he likes that it'll coincide with the end of the afternoon. He feels a rush of adrenaline when he realizes he needs to get home before night falls, or the mushrooms will incapacitate him.

One goes through the mountain, O thinks while he walks, slowly, confusing the butterfly with the orchid. The false division between the vegetable and the animal hurts us, and Trilcinea and I know that it's not easy to be in your head. The toilet is an extension of my ass, the pipes — my intestines and my urinary tract. My glasses, the TV, the screen on my computer are extensions of my eyes. The oven is an extension of my stomach. The houses in which I sleep and cook are my skin. The drugs are extensions of my dreams. Recorded music is an extension of my hearing that can hear around the world, even listening to the past. The bicycle, down to the tires, is an extension of my legs. The arrow is an extension of my fist. I like apples, I read books, chat with friends; I love. These things feed me, these things that pass through me. I metabolize, mix with others, only to be expelled, or, better yet, sent back, shared, but in another form, as though I were a blender.

He thinks/knows all of this, and I ask myself what all of this has to do with the orchid and the butterfly.

Obviously, he's hallucinating the relationships between colors, forms, and movements. If one sufficiently accelerates the time it takes an orchid to grow, of course it'll fly like a butterfly, and fly like the monarch butterflies that migrate from Canada to Mexico, as I told O. And while he walks through the forest like a crazy person, he thinks a mountain is a giant wave — that if you accelerate the movement of millions of years of solid ground on the earth and compress it into two minutes, you can see how the continents move, how solid ground is liquid, how a rock is a drop of water, foam, the mountains are waves, the external expression of a fast, yet subtle and, in the long run, insignificant movement in the tectonic plates. I'm a surfer on the mountain, he thinks/knows, and he laughs just to see how fucked up he is, and it's incredible how many different drugs he can take now, with so much practice, and still survive, function, enjoy. Any other person would hide under the covers and cry. And now the hours pass and he keeps walking around the mountain and now it's time to go home.

But seriously, O — is this really something to brag about right now? In everything you just thought there's a key. And he's happy to hear me.

And now you want me to take you seriously, Alice — now that I'm high as balls, on a mountain, several miles from town, and it's gonna get dark in a couple hours, and I could get lost. There are bears and mountain lions on this mountain, Alice.

If not now, when? You're gonna forget.

So do it, but let's talk while I run.

Pipes, prosthesis, orchid/butterfly, wave-mountain — there's a key there. Find it.

And how do you know?

I don't know. I'm in your head.

We've always been clear about that.

Of course. Well, let's see. If we play with the different temporalities of the prosthesis, the same thing happens that happened with the orchid/butterfly and the wave/mountain. The key is time. In so much as time is what makes us believe there are differences between things.

I try to help O.

Time is what's going to make me spend the night on this mountain while I trip on these mushrooms.

He gets frustrated. I help him. We'll we have to come up with the key quickly. Time isn't the key, but it's close. So come

43

on.

Ok. Let's speed up the prosthesis. If we do that, then the toilet doesn't look like a prosthetic of my ass. We can see the pipes being born in factories, moving, growing beneath the city, growing cement around them like membranes until finally the toilet comes out of the pipes and I come out of the toilet.

How does a city move? If we could see the growth of New York for three centuries in a two-minute video, what would it look like?

It would be an amoeba that evolves, or a technicolor flower that opens and expands. Or it could be a fetus growing in a woman's belly.

What kind of creature would the city be if we made its temporality compatible with ours?

It moves, grows, interacts, feels happiness, pain, contorts, devours, digests and shits, copulates and reproduces. It has a personality. It socializes and worries. How sad not to be able to see these things. How sad that we can't jump the box of time to see that we are little more than bacteria in the intestines of these titans, these gods.

We're doing well. I need to confirm this thought with O, validate it so he can keep going.

The key is that if we remove time as a factor then we can see everything as a prosthesis. The entire cosmos is our prosthesis, and everything is an extension of our powers. Starlight is a prosthesis of our gaze.

But, still, that's not it. It's too anothroponarcissistic. You're too slow. Don't use your ass as an example.

Shit, I'm getting distracted.

What's distracting you?

Well, you, Alice — you distract me.

Exactly — use that as an example.

Let's see. OK, so suppose that you're the butterfly and I'm the orchid. Or better that I'm the rock and you're the foam of the wave. Alice, I can barely see a thing; it's gonna be dark soon.

Trust the path you opened to lead you home. And think about me in this way, too. Do it. Let's think about you as a prosthesis and we'll shift time. What's happening? It's not so simple, right?

No. And I can't see anything. I'm getting kind of scared.

So wait. Catch your breath and wait until your eyes adjust to the dark. Ignore the hallucinations and think about the key.

If I come from the toilet, then you do, too. You and I come from the same plumbing. And everyone who shat there also came out of it at one time. You and I came out of the same plumbing, but that doesn't mean that you come out of me. Mixed guano. The mountain vibrates, Alice. I feel it in waves with my eyes closed. I see the waves.

You can't ignore the hallucinations anymore. Just enjoy them. Accept them for what they are, and continue with your assignments. The key and the path. There you go.

The key is that you might exist outside my head, that you probably wrote the obituaries, that the idea of "Alice" exists in others, with other names, that the celebration of the dead and the gravity that hurls us toward the concentrated history of their lives exists outside you, a plurality of existences, different worlds inhabited all at the same time, that even the mountain feels you as more than a someone — you're a movement, a move, a left hook that others have practiced.

Don't fall in the wolf den.

And this is how O falls down the den hole all the way to the cave of the old Romanian witch where he lands on his head with a terrible blow. He doesn't see the witch at first, but he perceives her presence in the cave and then she reveals herself. It's the witch who shows O his own obituary. There's a god, but he doesn't look anything like humans or animals. It's a god that we can only understand in minerals, in objects and their plasticity. Frankly, it looks more like a a machine made of metal and uranium. It's a cruel and indifferent god that couldn't care less about our extermination if, in the end, we are an anomaly of the atom, an anomaly of the object. The subject is an abnormal object.

O doesn't listen to her and reads the obituary with no small amount of pride.

Why does it say that I died in a Cathedral? he asks the witch.

She shows him the Cathedral and he believes he's there for three days. He sees me in the Cathedral. He walks up to me and gives me money.

It's everything I have, O says. I promise to send you more. Then he turns my gaze back toward the witch, as if to ask if he'll ever see me again.

Not everything's about you, my dear O, the old Romanian tells him, then says goodbye.

So much time spent waiting for the revolution, and now the revolution has happened, only nobody bothered to tell me, because nobody knew me, thinks/knows O. Everything beautiful is slow, he thinks and knows it, but if O doesn't wake up and manage to leave the cave he's going to die. Now Professor O neither thinks nor knows. In fact, when he falls into the cave he breaks his back and dies of asphyxiation. His funeral was in Puerto Rico. Alfred would rather not go. Trilcinea went, but didn't say a word. I went to pay my respects to O's devastated parents. I hadn't so much as introduced myself when his dad buried me in an octopus hug. I wanted to, but couldn't write an obituary. His mom got in touch a few days later to ask me to swing by the house. His dad was a writer, too. He ended up giving me O's computer at his mom's insistence. Who knows, maybe I looked like a daughter to her.

CHAPTER 3:
THE YEAR 2037

When Alice arrives in Brooklyn, the door of the house of the Artista Chilena and Professor Lagartija opens like a question: without greetings, or transitions, and with an energy that radiates from Alice's tiny body. Carrying suitcases bigger than she is, Alice only wants to say, ask, beg, plead: Tell me what happened!

There was a cacophony of questions at the port where she disembarked. Groups of three and four people had formed to exchange information, then split up never to see each other again and join another group, wanderers through an unexplored curiosity. Strangers beg one another for more information with an insatiable collective thirst to imagine. We're all children asking for explanations about how the universe works. The elders have that strange sensation — that emptiness before the abyss — that they will not be able to satisfy their curiosity before they die. People want to talk about what's just happened, and the opinion of everyone is important, not because it's an opinion, but because it's an imaginative catalyzer, a drug that we all deserve, that the world itself deserves after so much death and exhaustion.

We're still waiting for the official confirmation from NASA, yells Lagartijín from his room, peeking out from behind his computer for a second to say hello to his Aunt Alice who kisses, hugs, and dotes upon him in a way that only an aunt can — ("How big and handsome you are!", "Its'been too long!", "The girls must be crazy for you!", "Or the boys, I mean, for people your age it's better if it's *both*?!" etc.) — all synthesized in a quick and tender, "How wonderful to see you, Tijín."

Lagartijín excuses himself with half a wave and returns to his cave as quickly as he can to park himself in front of the only computer in the house, which he's monopolized for the past 10 years.

So, Lagartijín woke us up at 5:30 a.m with the news, said Profesor Lagartija.

And he was blind-drunk, says la Chilena, who's actually from Spain. We should do something about that, Lagartija.

She says it more out of formality than fear, Alice thinks/knows, smiling at her friend.

And the *stamina* that he has, the Professor continues. He got home from a rager at dawn. He'd taken all sorts of drugs, then wakes us up with the news and, without sleeping, spends the whole day glued to the computer reading every discussion forum he can find about The Contact.

Lagartijín interrupts the conversation with new information about ants. They're saying that the beings that contacted us made some kind of mistake, that the dominant species on the planet are actually ants, not us. And if we were like ants we would already have deciphered all the information that they sent us with our antennae. We wouldn't have needed to establish a common language, which is, precisely, the whole problem (Lagartijín, in his way, always wants to let the adults know that he's read his Kropotkin). How to find a common language with the other intelligent species of the galaxy that have already been conversing for millennia, if not millions of years before us. La Chilena likes the idea that we have to enter into a conversation *in medias res*, she says that it's like a game of jump rope where you have to find just the right moment to step in.

This is different from what we always imagined this moment would be, says Alice. We always thought it would be a direct contact with some alien being walking out of a UFO. And what we actually got is a coded message in mathematical language, a greeting or welcome to a galactic community that we've always seen, but never knew was actually there.

Lagartijín interrupts Alice to tell her that it's not a greeting, that the mathematicians and hackers in the online forums are saying that the message has a certain urgency, that they need something from us and that they need us to learn everything as quickly as possible.

But how are they communicating with us? How were they able to speak directly to the public and not to the government? Alice asks. Nobody knows.

Wikileaks was the first to report the news and the information went viral. Right there, on the only computer in the house, a 2019 Mac, they could read the entire message themselves. There in the living room, the conversation fills with silences. Every question and commentary gets long breaths that rise up to the ceiling followed by reflective eyes staring up through reflexive silences and cigarette smoke.

It's good that the information has gone viral so quickly, says Alice. The corporations can't manipulate it in their favor, or hide it.

Still, they're going to take advantage of the situation to militarize everything even more, replies Professor Lagartija.

Lagartijín barks a refutation from his room without getting up from the computer. With his back to the door so they can't see him, he snorts another line of blow to stay awake. He says that activist groups are already campaigning against militarization. The alien message makes it clear that none of the myriad populations that exists in the galaxy have been able to figure out how to travel faster than the speed of light. Physical contact and material exchange are unthinkable. The only possible form of contact over insterstellar distances is by way of radio waves. On the galactic level, all you can do is talk, and the only thing you can exchange are conversations. If we can't physically meet, nor exchange anything material, there's no need for any kind of military response, nor for any kind of economic transaction.

We can only talk! shouts the Chilena with no small amount of glee as she rolls a fat joint — clearly at the telepathic bidding of Alice of and Professor Lagartija, who're dying to think about The Contact through green lenses.

Only Lagartijín — who's on a whole other, much more intense, wavelength — declines to smoke. The conversation about a hyperpopulated galactic neighborhood of cultures (overpopulated? the Professor wonders) completely different from our own triggers an uncontrollable impulse to keep testing creative hythpotheses. The silences in their conversation gather and expand around the kitchen table — a scene that's playing out at that very moment in every other home around the world.

And they talk. And they talk more. And they smoke and keep smoking and share bottles of peach schnapps that Alice brought from Bolivia. And they talk about the possibility of a species that thinks in a collective or planetary manner. They talk about planets that are inhabited entirely by a single, global organism. They talk about black holes being the reproductive organs of universes that gather up genetic information and replicate it into other universes where it's born with tiny variations in its code, its laws of physics. Not without adrenaline or exhaustation, they contemplate the remote possibility that other galaxies in our universe might also be as populous as ours. And later they have pixilated conversations in which each speaker verbalizes a possibility instead of continuing that of another, externalizing their introspections, conversing in speculative punctuations, each one projecting a desire or fear that has more to do with us than with them.

And what if the blue aliens are capable projecting dreams onto reality?

What will their music be like? There's gotta be alien species with musical systems, and if not the blue aliens, definitely others.

Certainly there are aliens with technologies that allow them to control entire planets, manipulate stars, control the radioactive fields of solar systems.

I wonder if there are worlds where they fuck. It'd be good if fucking for pleasure were the common denominator among intelligent beings in the universe.

And what if millennia pass and we still don't understand one another? Millenia!

Maybe the most beautiful thing is that they've always been there and we didn't know. It would've been even more beautiful if we never knew, if we'd gone on passing like ghosts in the galaxy without knowing about them or them ever knowing about us, and then they discover our remains millions of years after we all die and mourn us.

(They hear a bark of disapproval from Lagartijín's room)

And what if they have an interstellar newspaper where they report the news of the galaxy?

Gossip about other worlds? Definitely.

They've definitely tried to communicate before. That message we received must've been sent a hundred years ago.

(We already know that! yells Lagartijín from his room. The message took 50 years to get here! And stop talking about them like they're only one group! There are many!!!)

They must be slow, move slowly. They're from another temporality based on another metabolism.

Exactly! It's the metabolism — how rapidly you convert ham into shit — that determines your temporality, the time.

Their metabolisms are slow and small, or slow and big, or fast, really fast, so fast that they live and die in two human seconds, which for them is an entire life.

And in this way worlds communicate with each other across generations. Every message will be answered by grandchildren or great grandchildren. At least it'll be this way with us.

(You're high! lectures Lagartijín, who's American, and looks Latin American, but speaks the Castillian Spanish of his parents. You can't just make shit up, kids. Quit fucking around and read what's being published in the forums! This is serious! *Serious*!)

We have to get back to sex. We're assuming there are generations, that they reproduce, that they even have sex.

Everything is alive. We're like the myriad species of bacteria that live in our stomach and help us digest. We live in the stomach of the galaxy, a universal metabolizer.

(Enough!)

And so, after a little while, as it happens with all news discussed among friends (who get high), they move on to more important subjects, they leave The Contact on the backburner and ask Alice about her travels, her projects. Professor Lagartija talks about the book he's writing, and the Chilena interrupts to show Alice, who she hasn't seen in 10 years, her new installation. While Lagartijín crashes on his bed and snores, they keep talking and drinking for hours. And every hour they get louder. They belly laugh, and wake Lagartijín who, resigned to not sleep because of the noise, joins the conversation while he makes coffee and lights one of his joints (because his weed is better than theirs), and the Chilena takes advantage of the opportunity provided by the fresh joint to ask Alice, at last, about Trilcinea.

Tijín pricks up his ears. He's been dying to hear about Trilci. Alice says Trilci got sick on the boat that they took through the Panama Canal from Puerto Rico, and, later, to Bolivia via Porto Arica.

Even though Trilci could barely eat when we arrived in Bolivia, everything with Tiago's connection worked out really well. They picked us up in La Paz and told us what they'd been doing while we were on our way to the mountains. Tiago, for his part, had told them about us, about our experiences in the school cafeterias, about our need to flee Puerto Rico. From the very first moment we met them they were clear that they didn't like what we'd been doing with drugs and the "faggots," nor could they imagine that we'd die happily for those reasons. But they wanted to work with us and share experiences anyway. Even though Trilci was sick, the first few weeks were amazing.

Alice and Trilcinea, with help from Tiago, had been smuggled out of Puerto Rico to a prison in Bolivia. A repurposed prison. A prison that resembled the Cathedral where they met Tiago. La Chilena, who intuits that Alice isn't ready to talk about Trilci, asks her how the whole cathedral/prison thing in Bolivia got started in the first place.

Well, it got started 20 years ago, before this whole shit show. Humanitarian groups were complaining about a Bolivian prison where children were living. A bizarre system of police corruption had allowed children to live there with their incarcerated parents. After a while, the police started allowing more and more of the outside world into the prison — vegetables, entire families, alcohol, etc. — all in such a way that the it became a kind of model prison precisely because of the corruption, not because they were trying to do the right thing. So, the humanitarian groups who came to volunteer were faced with a dilemma: denounce the prison and cut everything off — all the visits and food (things had been so bad before that there'd been a hunger strike where the prisoners had sewn their mouths shut), or look the other way. Not long afterward, the corruption turned into a kind of communal culture of coexistence and non-violence.

When we got there, Trilci and I suggested the introduction of *pijchado* (the Lagartijas have no idea what that is, but don't ask — Spaniards have imperial guilt, and they're always too embarrassed to ask when they don't understand Latin-American slang) to help get them off the *pasta base* (they don't know what that is either, but they're pretty sure it's crack). So, with some other *compañeras*, we did *acullis* (the Lagartijas contained their smiles, thinking it's marijuana, but then what's *pijchado*?) and would invite all the biggest *basuqueros* (crackheads?) to these informal *acullis* rituals as a substitute, though of course it should have been sorted out as a matter of policy and handled professionally because all we really managed to do was to get them high. Of course, they would've gotten high on anything, and even if you're a *basuquero* you can't go wrong with *aculli* and *ajtapi*! (oof!).

But we didn't realize that the situation in which we'd intervened was a kind of war between the *marihuaneros* and the *basuqueros*, because the latter would kill their own mothers to score while the *marihuanero* has his ethic. So it occurred to us to approach one of the old comrades of the Katarist guerrillas who was still in prison there and ask him how he thought we could keep the *pasta base* from killing them. What do you do? Denounce it and cut everyone off? Allow for corruption and become an accomplice of the mafia? Or use the corruption to create an ethical space that can, at the very least, promote some basic values? We made the food, prepared *acullicu*, and shared the oral history. But it was like fighting a dragon with a toothpick. It was child's play. So we began to focus on the kitchens.

None of the three Lagartijas said or asked anything.

This was a prologue, thinks/knows la Chilena. One invents prologues, makes them interesting, and converts the prologue into a book because the book hurts, and Alice wants to forget. Alice wanted to talk about other things — anything but Trilci.

And so, after only a couple of months there, both of us quite content, falling in love again, reborn after everything we lost in Puerto Rico, we find out that Trilci's dying, and there's no cure. She freaked out for the first couple of days, but then accepted it and began to see her death as an opportunity. She told our comrades at the prison that she'd come to die with them, to share her death happily, to invite them to happily accept the inevitability of their deaths and to use drugs for a happier life — all the knowledge we'd acquired in Puerto Rico at the happy death houses, which is to say: everything we learned on that goddamned island where the whole world was dying. And they all loved her. She worked every day in the common kitchens until a week before she died. I felt out of place after her death, walked around with lead feet for weeks, and then I just had to leave.

Professor Lagartija looks at Alice with his eyes and mouth wide open. He who always has so many words and knows how to listen and console wants to say something to comfort her, but he's so drunk that the words won't come. His face paralyzed and his brain sending contradictory messages, he begins to feel a twitch in his eyelids and stammers an eternal "uh" that never becomes a complete word.

I'm so sorry, says La Chilena, because sometimes that's enough. I'm so sorry. Sometimes those three words are a home, a refuge. I'm so sorry. And they're also a breeze.

Tijín, expert in changing the subject, in displacing the conversation to enter its medulla, like stacking all the furniture from the house in a single corner, asks Alice about the famine in Puerto Rico, and about Alfred.

Didn't news of The Great Famine make it to New York? Alice asks, then sees from the silent "No" on all three of their faces that it hadn't. (Upon hearing the words "great famine" for the first time now, Lagartija stretches out into his "uhhhhh." It's too much to process, and, with the exception of the young, men don't do well with consolation).

Well it's been going on now for almost 10 years. Alfred and I were in Santurce when it began, and Trilci lived nearby with her boyfriend. It was right after they killed El Jefe. All of a sudden, and with no alert, the military closed all the ports in the island and nothing got in or out, nor was there any way to leave the island. There was panic, of course. The military took over the schools and, pretty much anywhere they could, confiscated food, which effectively turned us all into beggars. They kept us in the city and wouldn't let anyone leave since the countryside and all agricultural production was now considered a matter of "colonial security." A lot of people began to die — quickly at first, and then more slowly. Children were the first to go. To avoid the spread of diseases, they'd kick the sickest outside of the city limits and just let them die alone. But they wouldn't let any of us who were healthy out. It was horrible for about four years. It's hard to know for sure, but based on the information we have it seems that about two-thirds of the population died during that time. It was by design that Puerto Rico didn't produce food before The Great Famine. It had been planned for decades. They knew in advance it was going to happen. We got scared that people might find out we had a cat in the house. People were eating cat on every corner. We understood; Alfred, the cat and I were all dying of hunger, too. But it was designed — a planned population reduction. They knew when oil began to run out that there were entire populations they could disappear with the press of a button, that they would have to use all of us to produce a massive surplus, and then starve us to death. They closed the ports and almost killed us all. They wanted to kill us all. That was the point. Either you die, or you join with the military as a slave, and many did, which was understandable. We couldn't. We continued to speak out, to protest, and to shit ourselves every time those motherfiuckers shot at us, which they always did. If it weren't for one of El Jefe's connections that he left for us before he got killed, chances are that none of us would've survived, at least not the three of us. Trilci's boyfriend lost hope and killed himself. Somehow we made it out of San Juan and wound up on the west coast with plans to flee to the Dominican Republic. Everyone said they had it better there than we did here, and that things had never been better in Haiti. The whole world wanted to go to Haiti in those days, and that was our plan when we left with El Jefe's maps. But when we arrived in the west, we decided to make contact with Tiago, El Jefe's connection, and we stayed in Isabela working in the happy death house. The hardest part about it is that when we were still in San Juan we had to keep the information El Jefe left us secret. The only person we shared it with was Trilci because the whole thing was so horrible that we decided to simply survive rather than run the risk that the military might find the secret paths out of the city, or that they might discover the mythical Cathedral in which we'd placed so much of our faith. I still have nightmares about it, about the huge number of people we indirectly killed in order to keep the information about the Cathedral secret. That blood is on our hands. And you know what? (At that point, the Lagartijas are afraid of what Alice might tell them next since the world she is describing — that terrifying, fucked up world — is completely foreign to them in their relatively protected life of New York. They are also furious. What Alice is describing may very well be their own future since the Caribbean has always been the future of the First World.) For some fucked up reason in my subconscious, I feel more more guilty for not having killed the cat and shared its meat with the children who were dying in my neighborhood, the babies of my neighbors, fucking Christ, who might have survived a few more days on the protein and fat of the cat we were hiding, than the irrefutable fact that we could've saved hundreds of lives if we'd shared the maps and connections El Jefe left us before he died. And it doesn't make sense, the whole thing with the cat, since we had a noble and anthropological excuse: he was one of us. And it wouldn't have saved anyone's life if we'd killed him; we'd have only prolonged the inevitable. But with El Jefe's connection we could've saved the lives of so many. And what tortures me in my nightmares isn't hiding the contact, it's hiding the cat. And what do I know? You can forgive yourself with time, I suppose, a little. Barely. Because that's one of the disastrous realities of life: that we forgive our own murderous acts.

The Lagartijas had no idea what Alice was talking about. She thought they understood some of it, but New York didn't know anything about what had really happened in the islands after they shut down the borders. The three of them sit with mouths wide open (the Professor practically convulsing from the shock of the information, not to mention the booze and the weed), and Alice grows tired of telling sad stories. Everything had been so sad — so spread out that one grows numb and tired. Alice thinks/knows that now she knows too many things.

To change the subject, Alice asks Tijín, in front of his parents, to please tell us what he's discovered about the aliens, though if he would first cut a line of that coke she saw him snorting in his room she'd be grateful.

Lagartija, who's still stuck in a paralysis between drunkenness and the desire to say something, gets so nervous that the *tic* in his eyelid synchronizes with an involuntary opening and closing of his lips, which makes it look like he's about to slobber.

La Chilena accepts that the truth is now out on the table, and that she, too, could use a line.

Lagartijín is more than happy to oblige, and gives them his hypothesis about the aliens. The latest in the forums, he tells them, is that the alien message contains various things about genetic manipulation and that it's full of a drawing of the double helix, but it's a genetic sequence that doesn't seem to have any correlation whatsoever with our biology.

Don't be so fucking square, Tijín! Alice tells him. Speculate! Tell us what you want the message from the aliens to be.

Tijín accepts her invitation. He understands that his elders, vampires of youth, need their fantasies. They need to renew themselves with their fictions, and that makes them feel equal parts sadness and solidarity.

I believe that Tiago's fractal Cathedral has the answer to

the question the aliens are asking. I think they're proposing an objective, a goal that will unite us. They're giving us the mathematical keys to reproduce the universe, to help us create other universes, little Big Bangs. The genetic codes they're giving us have nothing to do with biology. They're telling us that we are, in reality, genes, and that the laws of physics in our universe, imperfect as they are, lie inside our brains. They can give us the formula to reproduce universes very much like ours so that we can extend ourselves as offspring of atoms into universes similar to ours, but different — universes that have the minimum conditions for intelligent life to emerge in new forms. Without a doubt, the message of this first contact is that our universes must copulate.

Lagartija's *tic* twitches when he hears his son elaborate this sustainable fantasy, a desire that reaches beyond the constraints of reality. He's happy. His son's fantasies are like an oniric helicopter. And he falls half-asleep, snoring with a smile on his face, half-conscious, falling without the fall. Alice and La Chilena keep talking to Tijín, doing lines. They put music on and dance their tits off until the sun is well on its way across the sky. Then the three old friends sleep together in the same bed while Tijín gets ready for work.

And the days pass. Alice works with La Chilena in the schools, Lagartija at the university. Tijín studies in the morning and, in the afternoon, rescues food in the city that he delivers to one of the centers where La Chilena works. The conversations about the aliens multiply. Strangers keep talking. And for the first time in years, New York is full of hope.

Then one day the conversation gets interrupted when the military police take over the food rescue center to draft Lagartijín along with thousands of other young people for compulsory military service. Tijín dies in the middle of a battle in Texas in which he refuses to shoot. What his parents don't know is that Tijín had stolen a mountain of programs and information that he sent to Tiago at the Cathedral in Puerto Rico, and that with that information, a fledgling new world would be born while the husk of the old world rots. Lagartijín was the first to send a message to the blue aliens, though they wouldn't receive it for another 50 years. The conversation would last for centuries.

After Tijín's death, and the death of hundreds of other young people kidnapped for a war that doesn't exist, it's the mothers of the sons of the first contact who bravely take to the streets. But La Chilena doesn't find solace in the streets now. She's sick of death, plagued by death. Her dead son is just one more link in a chain of deaths she can't bear. More from exhaustion than sadness (though she's drowning in sadness), she plans her final work of art. For months she keeps it hidden from Lagartija and Alice. In secret, she plans a campaign of silence for the last Friday in March to honor the dead whose lives are the cost of electric light. It begins as a simple act of civil disobedience in which anyone can participate. And on that Friday, the people observe silence. They wake up to a newscast where the producers, courageously, decide that the broadcast will be nothing more than an hour of the anchors on screen observing silence. The teachers join together and the schools are silent. In the subway full of commuters: silence. At night the bars are like monasteries — crowded with drunks in silence, drunks who don't utter a fucking word.

Later, La Chilena proceeds with the second step. At midnight on that same night, the earth will turn off. For months she's studied how to sabotage the electrical grid in the last illuminated city in the world, the final super-parasite on the planet. And when the date arrives, the earth will go dark for a whole weekend, the first silence of light in 150 years. She'll quiet the earth to honor the dead. After the night of silence, Alice and Lagartija never hear from La Chilena again.

Alice lives with Lagartija in Brooklyn for a few more years. They write. They write like banshees. They write as if the world is about to end and writing is the only thing that can save it. And in a very real way, the world is ending. Twelve books between the two of them. Twelve books in three years that are really letters. Not to the coming generations, but to the coming world, to the world that will follow — the world in which they know they can't live. In the year 2040, following Trilcinea and Alfred's instructions for a happy death to the letter, they end their lives together. And so, without even knowing it, and surrounded, alone, by death, they discovered one of those disastrous realities of life: Only ruins and words survive disaster.

CHAPTER 4:
THE YEAR 2701

The heart of a bird beats every .02 seconds. That of a human, every .7. A blue whale: every minute. And in the same manner, the heart of a city beats twice a day. The universe's heart beats at least twice every 26 billion years (being the expansion of the Big Bang and it's corresponding contraction, the Big Crunch). A single organism, multiple and dynamic, with each individual acting as a neuron in a giant brain. While each individual has slightly different genetic material, that information is easily accessed by the brain. It's for that reason that the digital era didn't last. It's purpose for the brain was to be a mirror — the brain came to know and exteriorize itself, making itself virtual. All that information stored digitally turned out to be nothing more than a miniscule reflection of the information stored in our cells. We just had to learn the digital language so we could decipher the language of our genetic code. And we understood ourselves in the end like genes that transport the information necessary for reproduction. Only then did The Boxing Smurfs arrive.

II

Moved, perhaps, by the nostalgia that produces the petrification of the Smurfs, one girl named Alicia, from the Trilce region in the Atacamia zone, proposed to go back through the 14 books from the beginning of the millenium that the regional library kept on hand. She remembered from her classes in historical imagination that in that time period they made many copies of the same book, that after The Great Plateau happened, it had been decided that one copy of each book would be enough to maintain a reference library of that epoch, and that all other superfluous copies were torn apart and turned into radioactive trash in the desert. Every region around the world kept between 6 and 24 books from this epoch, each copy unique, because for a book to be read one time by anyone was enough for all to understand it. Somewhere in the 14 books, she remembered vaguely by intuition or induction, there was a key to the Smurfs that had perturbed her. She abandons her meditations, grabs a couple of pears, and leaves on her radiosensing umbrellacycle, bouncing along the radiation waves all the way to the library.

Atacamia has underground vegetable gardens in caverns like wolf dens with artificial light extracted from the high levels of radiation in the desert above. In fact, the radiation is so high on the planet's surface that life can only be sustained when it's shielded from the sun. The plants that remain — more violet than green — grow in domes and mega-gazebos covered in solar panels that repel the rays of the sun. And while floating on her radiosensing umbrellacycle, the Alicia can see the whole region of Atacamia lit up by the reflection from the anti-radiation solar panels. Where there's no cover, everything is red mud. There in Atacamia, life survives in caves and cupolas.

At the library, she goes back over the 14 books she read when she was a little girl. She only finds one reference to the Smurfs in a book that seems to be either poetry or history, but it doesn't say anything about their origin. The title of the book is *La dignidad*, and it's written in pre-Plateau Spanish.

III

We know that for centuries the earth was inhabited by angels — beautiful, solitary, and, ultimately, mortal beings. The angels sang songs about heroes that their listeners already knew, that their listeners changed over the centuries. And since the dead don't have names, they named them. The angels were the sole ruin, resistant superstitions, of a lost world. And they took up residence in the abandoned cathedrals. We didn't really understand what a cathedral was, but sometimes, curious, we would attend just to listen to the intoxicating songs that came from the light of the angels. That was when the blue aliens arrived, the boxing Smurfs. Some of us believed that they'd arrived from the unexplored depths of the ocean while others believed they were intergalactic travelers. They didn't seem to be a threat. They were tiny. They lived in some other, much slower, spacetime. It could take them weeks just to move a hundred meters. Neither animal nor vegetable, they photosynthesized, barely drank water, had huge brains in relation to the size of their bodies, and wore little red hats and gloves. The radiation didn't effect them at all. In fact, they were the only living being on earth that could travel the great desert without the protection of an umbrella. It was said that their red, mushroom-shaped hats protected them from the effects of the radiation. Over a long period of time they went about the planet, drawn to the angels, attracted, it seems, by their light. With their vegetable slowness, they gathered around the cathedrals where the angels lived. They surrounded them, blocking even a single ray of the angel's light from escaping, which reproduced and petrified the Smurfs' static forms and made them part of the cathedral in symbiosis with the trapped storyteller angels that could never leave. All they could do was sing beautiful obituaries, their name-giving baptisms. For 60 years it's been impossible to enter the cathedrals. But the loss should not be lamented. Those of us who don't die, who are the river of the Milky Way, don't need to mourn the cathedrals. We who love what's lost (because what's lost is always our future) should understand that those cathedrals will inevitably return without any effort whatsoever on our part. But the same compassion shown to us, the same care that keeps and maintains us, the same galactic commune with which we have symbiotized, inevitably fills us with nostalgia, which is to say: hunger for the future.

IV

Among the final songs/obituaries we heard the angels sing before The Boxing Smurfs' petrifying obsession sealed the cathedrals was the song/obituary of one Acteón Pacquiao, a modern fighter who combined the fluidity of an imperceptible attack and the power of a smile as interchangeable as modes of speed or entropy. It was the magic of what he couldn't understand. Who could create entropy with a smile? Our only weakness is our fascination with what we don't understand, the perturbing fascination that draws this Alicia to the library. Our reasoning is effective. Which is to say, the incomprehensible is determined more by our stupidity than by our interest, and our weakness is our interest in what we don't understand. That's to say: Our weakness was the Smurf's interest in the angels in the cathedrals that sang the obituaries of forgotten heroes, which we could no longer hear nor see.

V

And so we begin to experiment with the jail/cathedral that the blue creatures had made to trap the light from the song of the angels. Smurfs secrete certain oils. Taking this drug makes us slower, more introspective, but not much unhappier. When we take it, we reconnect with the biological universe of our internal organs. We construct little jail-cathedrals inside ourselves. When we lick the oils in the folds of the petrified Smurfs, we prefer to concentrate more on the blood coursing through our veins than the water in our rivers; on masturbation more than orgy.

And this is how we arrived at a terrible conclusion: The Smurfs are the substance of which we're all made. The Smurfs are a river that carries us away, but we're the river; they're a tiger that mauls us, but we're the tiger; they're the drug that we take, but we're the drug. The Smurfs are happily real; we, happily, are not.

VI

The Alicia licks so much Smurf that, one day, they believe she's one of them and open a small hole for her to enter the cathedral. Inside, she floats in another atmosphere without gravity, the giant cathedral with its columns that rise to the ceiling covered in blue Smurf faces and bright red boxing gloves. She floats in the green light of the angel and dances to the rhythm of its song about a soldier named Inca Valores who had a second face on his chest that delivered lectures while he slept. There in the anti-gravity, the Alicia flies while she dances with the angel, uses her arms like wings, and zigzags between the columns until she arrives at the roof. Then she plunges down again noticing that there are tiny cracks in some of their boxing gloves from which little droplets of milk seep. The angel stops singing for a moment and gets drunk on the milk. The Alicia does the same, and she's happy, and she never wants to leave the cathedral again. She stays four months without leaving the cathedral even once, and only then, in the green light of the angel, does her obituary arrive. The Smurfs are going to kill everyone just like they're killing me. It's fine that they're exterminating us. Everything is just fine.

CHAPTER 5:
THE YEAR 2033

He sits in the window and stares at the sea. He can practically taste the fish in the saltwater breeze. Two hours later he moves to the opposite window. He sees the mountains, smells the river, and tastes the vegetable emanation on the wind. Now he watches iguanas and monkeys. In the afternoon they climb the mountain to look for shelter and fresh water. He stares out the window with the certainty that everything he sees belongs to him.

We're protected now, he thinks/knows. *The unilateral decision made by the gigantic hairless cats in my group to move us to this new enclosure wasn't bad. Not bad at all. There's more food here, and I don't have to be afraid of the bigger cats with their endless appetites where we lived before. Regardless, they should've consulted me.*

He senses the presence of Alice as she moves behind him and gently scratches his back.. He turns his gaze and looks her directly in the eyes. It's not recrimination. He nuzzles her nose in a gesture of approval.

She's got an authoritarian streak, he thinks/knows, *but she's still my cat. Of course all of this would come unraveled without me.*

He hadn't worked so hard since they moved from the urban Santurce to the sparsely populated seaside town of Isabela. His labors are imperative: *I keep watch at the windows while the others hunt; I keep rodents out of the cupboards even though there's less food to guard (and, frankly, I prefer the rats); I keep myself clean, stretch, meditate, and sleep for 20 hours a day. Sleeping all day with 12 dying people in the rooms next door is no easy task. The smell of death doesn't bother cats. It's part of life. And those dying are the best — kind and easygoing. They sleep a lot, too. They only get up to stretch, eat, and pet us. Correction: My work is to be beautiful so that the dying can enjoy me, to assist them in dying the happy death that my cats — Alice, Alfred, and Trilcinea — preach despite the fact that they're the only ones who disturb the peace in this house. They are always moving. They barely sleep. They come and go all day long, moving things from one place to another, inexhaustible creators of chaos.*

And the cat moves from room to room, being sure to take at least a 30-minute nap with each one of the dying. All of them pet him in a different, yet complimentary way.

They pet me and they love me, even as they die. I'm beautiful. So beautiful. I must be a god.

Both his eyes and his nose tell him that Alfred's brought a lot of cod when he comes through the door. He runs to greet him, be beautiful and shake him down for fish. Afred is weak. He always gives the cat whatever he asks for. A mollycoddler at heart, he's nevertheless always felt that the cat gives him so much more than he gives the cat, and so he gives him cod and spoils him. The cat gave him back his sanity during a time of great pain. Alfred looks worried. His skin is tan. He goes to sleep thinking about all the problems, the little things, the responsibilities. He's only calm when he smokes or cooks. He moves rapidly, takes the cod to the kitchen. He gives Alice a peck on the cheek, looks for the potatoes in the tray. He arranges the fish, then takes out the knives to filet and mince them. Alice synchronizes her movements with Alfred's. They've been cooking together for many years. They used to discuss and debate the ingredients of every dish, and sometimes fight. There was a heavy French influence on her cooking, and Alfred hated the French. To Alice, on the other hand, Alfred was practically a savage in the kitchen, almost entirely lacking subtlety and attention to detail. But after years of practice, and particularly after the famine, it's as though their culinary minds had become one — complimentary hemispheres. They move without talking because they don't need to, because in the kitchen they communicate better than in any other situation. In the kitchen, they simplify their worries, put them in perspective, and forget them. Feeding people is always more important, more vital, than their worries. When she sees the huge quantity of cod that Alfred brought, Alice looks for a block of salt and a scale, then starts salting the filets to dry and preserve them. Today they're going to make a Portuguese *bacalhoada*. They hadn't decided to make it beforehand. Alfred didn't know he would find so much cod at the coast. They hadn't discussed it. It was just obvious that if you find that much cod and you have to cook for 15 people that the most obvious thing to make is a *bacalhoada*, which will allow them to stretch the diminishing supplies of potatoes, onions, peppers, and tomatoes that might otherwise go bad. Alice salts half of the cod. It seems like too much to Alfred, but he trusts her as she disappears for a moment out onto the patio.

In the window, the cat looks down at one of the chickens with scorn. Alice comes back with a handful of eggs to compliment the protein of the cod. The cat watches them from the kitchen window, enjoying the spectacle of Alice and Alfred's synchronized movements, the warmth and smells they generate. He's full now, but keeps eating everything Alfred tosses to him. They light the stove, boil the potatoes and the eggs in sea water. After they take them out, they chop the onions, peppers and tomatoes and mix them in with the minced cod in six pans with a lot of oil. And there, in that dance of his cats, in that ordered chaos of lovers who don't even have to speak to feed us all, and which elevates them above their anxieties — there in the kitchen, in that silence full of sounds and smells, they reach, produce, a space of peace in a house full of death.

They put the pans in the oven. Only then does Alfred take a deep breath and invite Alice to accompany him to a gathering of the communes on the coast. There's unrest among the people, rumors that the military want to charge them a food tax now that supplies are low in San Juan and Guaynabo, rumors of a faction that blames the death house for drawing unnecessary attention to their black market supplies, and that they should withhold resources from the dying to combat the false impression that they have more food than they need.

Alice doesn't want to. They'll have to flee. It's inevitable. Better to take their training in the arts of happy death and abscond with the knowledge. And anyway, she can't confide in Alfred anymore. She still loves him without the slightest regret, but he's crazier than a mechanical rat now. Crazy and insufferable. She has other plans, secret plans for tonight: She'll take Alfred, Trilci and the cat and try to find the mysterious Cathedral they've heard so much about and make a connection that can take them to Haiti where, they say, since the oil crisis, things have never been better. The rest of the world dying of famine and the Haitians are thriving, so much so that they have to defend their border with the Dominican Republic.

Alfred goes to the gathering alone. The cat naps with Colonel Carlos, a very sick old man who can barely get out of bed. Colonel Carlos can only find peace in morphine and the company of a feline.

Work in the kitchen never ends. There won't be dinner tonight, but Alice takes out eggs, limes, sugar cane, and cheese.

The front door opens once again. The cat doesn't get up, but stretches out on Carlos' bed as though to say, *Wake up — it's gonna be good.* Trilci comes in and the last light of vespers spills in through the doorway. The cat associates Trilci with the smell of pot, and the smell of pot with catnip, and the catnip with the good feelings and good humor of the dying gathered in the living room to smoke and tell stories, to distract themselves from their pains while Alice cooks a precarious lime cheesecake. Colonel Carlos crosses his fingers in hopes that there might be a line or two of coke, which has gotten scarce.

When Carlos smokes he gets creative. He's a deserter from the American Army where his years of service made him crazy. When Alice arrived in Isabela with El Jefe's maps and documents two years ago, she was looking for a man named Tiago, who, El Jefe had said before he died, lived in a cathedral with resources to support and protect many people. She never found Tiago, but she found Carlos who knew Tiago and had been distributing supplies from the Cathedral to the surrounding death homes. The Colonel, nevertheless, was paranoid and suspicious, and wouldn't put Alice, Alfred and Trilci into direct contact with Tiago or the people at the Cathedral. A few years earlier, during The Great Famine, the Colonel was traumatized by the overwhelming number of people who died when the military confiscated all the resources. That was when he'd decided to desert, but not without first stealing dozens of containers of medical supplies, canned food, construction materials, and pallets full of morphine and coke, which he stored at the Cathedral. And so, when he began to die, he proposed to Alice that they make a happy death home, that his contact at the Cathedral would ration the stolen supplies back to them, and that their happy death home wouldn't lack for food, drugs, and medicine. They could do something amazing with all of it, give hope to the people who'd begun to recover from the disaster of The Great Famine. It wouldn't be a hospital. They wouldn't be there to cure people. It would be more like an ongoing death party.

This scares Alice a bit. What they're doing isn't an insurgency nor a guerrilla operation, but she knows that the military brass doesn't like having the death houses around, and that they're always waiting for the any excuse to shut them down.

And when you die, Carlos, how will we get the supplies to keep running this happy death house?

The cat, Alice — the cat knows all my secrets. Ask the cat when I die.

It seems like a joke, but somehow she knows it isn't. Carlos spends hours talking to the cat. And the cat listens to him. The cat looks the Colonel in the eyes when he pontificates on the fractalist groups and the clandestine biocentric Cathedral.

Carlos respects me, the cat thinks. *Alice is still my favorite, Trilci always has good vibes, Alfred is sweet and spoils me with fish, but the Colonel respects me and speaks to me without using an idiot baby voice. He calls me Mandelbrot, he says, because, though I'm fat in the middle, he admires my fractal beauty. It's because I'm so beautiful, have I told you?*

The dying gather in the living room to smoke Trilci's pot. The cat runs to her and begs his catnip, which Trilci gladly gives him. Everyone relaxes in the smoke-filled room while the cat runs from window to window with demented intensity. Carlos begins to talk about the divisions between the various fractalist groups. The cat already knows these stories, but since the Colonel always tells them when everyone's completely stoned, they always forget, and so they always want to hear them again the next time they're stoned.

The first fractalists postulated that all the galaxies we can see in the universe are a reflection of our own solar system from other times, that the universe is a bubble of projected images that bounce off the walls of the universe and infinitely multiply the same light and the same objects, but at incalculably different times. In other words, they think there's only one galaxy, but repeated infinitely from its own projection, and that we are, down to our atoms, reflections of our galaxy, that everything is inside and outside of everything else.

In other words, Carlos, you're saying you're inside me a whole bunch of times.

Of course, my dear Trilci, you make it so much simpler.

Trilci likes to poke fun at Carlos so he'll flirt back with her. She likes to give that pleasure to the dying old coot who can't get it up anymore because of the huge quantities of morphine he takes, though the first thing he'd do if he could would be to jack off thinking about her. Trilci feels tenderness for him. Trilci and Alfred let him watch when they have sex. Not Alice, though. Alice doesn't trust Carlos. And though she wouldn't admit it, she resents Alfred and Trilici's love affairs. Not because of Alfred, with whom she'd fallen out of love a long time ago. She still loves him, but it's something different. In the past few years, Trilci's the only one for whom Alice feels any desire. Alfred always said that when they got to Puerto Rico something fundamental changed in Alice. Before, she'd loved love, literature, and cooking, and saw those social acts as more or less solitary and domestic. But once she got to Puerto Rico, she began to develop a passion for the clan, the tribe.

It's that she killed the angel when she arrived on the island, Alfred, Trilci tells him.

Trilci noticed the change, too. Trilci, as though she understood this nonsense, took that angel — that mysterious heroic character Alice had always talked about — and appropriated it, turned it into something evil, into the nemesis of Alfred's Smurfs.

We're cyclical, Carlos continues like a preacher. The only thing we'll find in the galaxies is the past and the future of earth trapped in a bubble. When the fractalist physicists made this discovery there was great sadness, a tranquil sadness among the fractalist groups. But it was a liberating sadness, especially now that they think the world is ending. But in all of the groups there are desperate optimists.

Like this cat, Trilci interrupts. Trilci loves to interrupt Carlos' nonsense. See how much he loves to run around all crazy on drugs?

All eyes land on the cat with smiles.

I love when they watch me. It's because I'm so handsome.

And he knows that we're dying," says one of the dying women. "We smell of death, and he knows.

You smell like good people, Trilci replies. You smell of love and life.

They're dying, I'm dying, we're all dying.

But the cat knows that it's OK, that it's a good thing. According to Carlos, we're not dying, we're rebounding, and that's better.

Exactly, says Carlos, and takes the opportunity to continue. That's precisely the problem among the two camps of fractalists. The first say, naively, that everything is fractal, that the fractal is the law of everything, that we're fabric more than we're space-time, a membrane of interdependent scales, communicated in the vibrations, in the rebound, in frequencies of gravity. The second group of fractalists emerged from the first, and they say that, in effect, fractal was everything, but only because we perceive everything as a fractal. All our perceptions of the universe, and all our senses utilize the fractal as a mode of organizing information. We live our lives trapped in the empire of this form because we can't perceive anything without it. The fractal isn't real, it isn't in the universe; it's an anthropological question that organizes the perception of the universe. So the second wave fractalists believed in the necessity of breaking away from the fractal forms, in terms of perception, in order to finally enter the universe.

Carlos, always the storyteller, keeps telling and telling his strories of the fractalists even though he keeps losing his listeners who keep starting their own stoned side conversations. It occurs to Trilci that maybe it would be a good idea to get out paper and pencils so the dying can draw fractals, which is a lot of fun. You just choose a form and repeat it in fractals, and nobody understands it. Someone asks the Colonel if he'll show us the fractals that he's always talking about, and everyone gets excited. The more irregular, the more beautiful they turn out. Everything's a question of perseverance, of repeating the same image at different scales like a mantra.

And night falls because nights don't arrive; they fall. (In another time, Professor O would have said the days turn off.)

But now Alice comes alive. She waits for Alfred to return from the assembly before serving the lime cheesecake. It took her three weeks to get all the ingredients, and not without help from the Colonel's secret contacts.

Alfred announces that he was able to trade the few remaining gallons of gas to the neighboring commune for a kilo of coke, and everyone who's still awake gets excited. Alice already knew. Under his breath, Alfred tells her that things got ugly at the assembly, that the neighboring communes either hate or fear the death houses, that they have to do something soon.

In the middle of the party — everyone's shitfaced now since Alice put tons of concentrated marijuana oil in the lime cheesecake — Alice sneaks into Carlos' room. The Colonel is tying himself off to shoot up his morphine. Alice climbs on top of him and shows him her tits. Finally. The Colonel is happy.

Carlos, you have to give me your contact for the hidden Cathedral, and you have to give it to me now, Alice says as she strokes his hair.

The Colonel, completely unperturbed and trying without

success to get it up, tells her again not to worry, that when he dies the cat is going to tell us how to find the contact. Alice wants to believe him, but it's not the point.

We're leaving *tonight*, Carlos, *papito*, and I need you to tell me right now, and in great detail, how to contact Tiago and the people at the Cathedral. You're too weak to keep going there. I don't give a fuck about the cat. I believe you, and because I believe you I have a lethal dose of morphine and, right now, I'm stronger than you. If you don't tell me, I'm going to inject you and you're going to die tonight. But if you tell me, then I'll make sure you get all the food and drugs all twelve of you need to keep partying until you die. I've been taking care of you for two years. You know you can trust everything I say to you. You can trust that I'll keep my word if you give me the contact as much as you can trust that I will kill you right now if you don't. All twelve of you may be dying, but Alfred, Trilci, the cat, and I are all healthy and alive.

Don't take the cat, Alice. You can't leave me without the cat, the Colonel begs.

Oy, Carlitos. You're so charming. You know how much we love you. But you also know what a fucker you've been — keeping your contact for the supplies secret to keep us tied here. All we want is a chance to get to Haiti, a chance to survive. You know how the military is, and you know they're going to kill us the minute they find an excuse.

Carlos grabs Alice's tits, then starts to cry. He tells her everything she has to do to contact Tiago from the Cathedral.

Alice, having already packed everything necessary for Trilci and Alfred, convinces them they have to leave immediately while the dying are wasted on the lime cheesecake. There's no time to lose. The dying have enough salted cod and other necessary supplies to last weeks until they send more from the Cathedral. Alfred and Trilci, who trust Alice with their lives, follow her lead without question.

After a four-hour walk in the dark, having only looked back once at the illuminated windows of the happy death house where their twelve dying friends were enjoying perhaps the greatest party of their lives, they arrive at the Cathedral. It isn't in the mountains like they'd thought, but in a series of caves hidden in the cliffs overlooking the sea. They're greeted by an old Romanian woman to whom they say, "Smurfs and fractals" — the first passcode the Colonel gave them. The old Romanian lives in the caves below, caves that are like the entryway of the Cathedral, and she hosts them and the cat there for the night.

The cat is deathly afraid. The cave is full of butterflies. The deafening sound of the wave stuns and disorients him. He's paralyzed, the poor feline, with stress. Alfred, Alice and Trilci rise with the first light and the sight of the sea from the caves in the cliffs overwhelms them with its immensity. The old Romanian shows them the secret stairs that will take them to the Cathedral. Once they get to the top of the stairs, they'll have to give the second passcode, she tells them, then asks for the name of their contact.

Tiago, they say.

At the top of the stairs they marvel that there's electricity in the cave. And the further in they go, the more butterflies there are. They never could've imagined what they see next. The Cathedral is an elaborate, hidden city made of tunnels connected to giant central spaces with light holes in the ceiling and smaller spaces with natural windows that look out onto the sea. It's full of kids and teenagers and a handful of old people, and it extends through miles of cliffs on the northeast coast of Puerto Rico.

They see giant tubes that descend to the bottom of the sea. They see a central room where the ceiling of the cave reaches up 300 feet to where the sunlight comes in through a circular dome made of stained glass in the shape of an enormous yellow, green, and red orchid. It's full of butterflies and innumerable species of plants that cling to the cracks and crevices above. They see dozens of adolescents and children working on computers, programming tireless machines and robots that shape the interiors of the Cathedral or travel through the tubes to the bottom of the ocean and return with food. They see the handful of older people organizing libraries. They see an interactive map of the world on a dark screen that shows data on supplies and resources moving throughout Latin America. They see unending networks of wheels, wires, valves, crystals, containers, and apparently infinite subterranean tunnels that lead to laboratories, metal workshops, and mining cars that barely make a sound and seem to be conveyed by electromagnetism. They see the inner workings of underground abundance beneath the surface of a world shaped by scarcity. And with barely a word between them, Alice, Trilci and Alfred all feel the sad and beautiful fortune of being witnesses to a future that doesn't need them.

The old Romanian leads them through the endless tunnels, deliberately disorienting them so that they don't know how to leave. It's not that they don't trust them, these strangers, but that it's part of the protocol that explicitly instructs them not to trust anyone of their age. There, one can only trust in the young and the old. The three of them are full of questions, but the visual marvel of each space leaves them speechless.

Tiago works in the next room, which has a beautiful view of the ocean, says the old Romanian. He will answer your questions.

Tiago, it turns out, is a 13-year-old boy. This doesn't surprise any of them. He seems more mature than his age, but everyone there is. Tiago gets excited when he sees the terrified cat in his basket.

I have an idea, he says to them without introducing himself. There are some big windows in the next room, some chamomile, and a little lime tree. We can let the cat out there. He'll love it. There are lots of butterflies.

Tiago takes him out of his basket and the cat runs to hide with its face in the chamomile plant.

I'm not prepared for another move. What kind of torture have my captors planned for me?

Tiago opens a clam and offers it to the cat who looks to Alice for approval.

Alice gave me the nod, so let's see what this Smurf has to offer.

Everyone sits around the little lime tree and takes in the enormity of the ocean. They have questions, but they don't know where to begin. Besides, Tiago seems more interested in the cat than in them.

Alfred wants to ask about the electricity and the machines. How is this possible if the military has all the petroleum left in the world?

Trilci wants to ask about the stained glass dome with the orchid on the ceiling in the central room of the Cathedral. She wants to ask why there are so many children, where they're from, what they're doing, and what the data on the map of the world means. Always the optimist, she wants to believe that they've finally made contact with the global revolution.

Alice, always suspicious, would like to know what's going to happen to them now that they've seen the whole hidden Cathedral there in the cliffs? She suspects that they won't let them leave, that they now know too much, which is never good. But the three of them ultimately say nothing, ask nothing, and arrive at their own conclusions.

The old Romanian tells me you have the Colonel's passcode. Is Carlos dead? He helped us so much at the beginning, and it pains me that we couldn't cure his condition. The last time we spoke with him he told us many good things about you three — that you truly cared about the people at the happy death house, that the dying could enjoy the rest of their lives there. But you must have so many questions, no?

The three heads nod without saying a thing. The cat bats his eyelashes.

If I make myself beautiful, the Smurf will give me another clam.

Well, this place is one of many "cathedrals" as you call them, spread throughout the world. Though we haven't been able to connect with them all, the ones we know about are all different from one another, but united by various principles on which we almost all agree. We have two missions, the first of which is to build a world that works — an economy based on resources, not money. For that we calculate our resources using all versions of a software that gets updated daily to calculate our resources based on our biological priorities. We're all mechanical engineers and programmers. The machines do all the work.

Tiago, 13, carries himself like an adult with excellent manners, the vocabulary of a professor, and the intelligence of a mathematician.

Trilci's charmed by this, and wants to eat him up.

Alice, always paranoid, remains suspicious. Children who skip their adolescence become cruel when they're adults.

Alfred believes he's hearing Smurf voices again and he's about to scream to shut them up, but resists the urge. He looks around in every direction and listens to this strange being who seems to be too eloquent, not for his age, but for this world of pure delirium.

The second mission is to assist people who are dying with their transition into death. And that's where the death houses and what Trilici called "happy death" came in. We were thrilled when the Colonel told us that "happy death" was what you called it. We've borrowed your concept in many of the Cathedrals, Trilci. You're famous without even knowing it. The thing is, kids,... (The kid calls us "kids"!) ...this paradigm of overproduction of oil, in which every year we must triple the production of the previous year so that the present can simply function, always in debt to the future, has been based in the permanent overproduction of children — each year the planet becoming more overpopulated than the last. So we knew that many people would die during this transition. We're in the hangover period. We've learned to live in solidarity with the dying, to help them with their deaths. The elders who come here to live with us teach us compassion, that compassion is the key to world we're creating. But there are people — confused people — who are opposed to compassion. And the best way to teach compassion is to practice it in the death houses, assisting in happy death, which is nothing more than creating a space for those who suffer to have dignity.

Now it's Trilci who's suspicious of what Tiago says.

To Alice, meanwhile, it makes perfect sense. This idea gives her peace. To accept the death of so many without rendering their lives meaningless, to give it meaning — only happiness can give it this meaning. And this city of children in the Cathedral has a better chance of being happy than her decadent generation does.

Alfred, for his part, is about to have a nervous breakdown. A cold sweat and the vertiginous view of the sea from the cave aren't helping any.

The cat comes out of his hiding place and presents himself with confidence. He smells and inspects Tiago, then decides to hunt butterflies.

That's why almost all of us here are children. Not all of the Cathedrals have adopted this idea. Surely you've seen this concept played out in Darwinian, apocalyptic films, no? Who should survive and who should die? This isn't the point for us. We want to build something that distributes resources for all, and for this reason, it was better to start with children who are exiled from the capitals and sent to die every day. We only assimilate children younger than 10. I arrived here with El Jefe when I was only 7 years old. El Jefe rescued me when they killed my parents. I knew him because my mom was a teacher and my father was an engineer. They started working with El Jefe on this project 20 years ago.

And on go the stories of Tiago, with varied reactions from his listeners. He tells them that they can't really use solar and wind energy because the military would almost certainly find them right away. But they're protected by the cliffs and get all the power they need from the sea, from the violence of the waves. They'd put a kind of pendulum weighing several tons on a floatation device in the water. It generates electricity with the waves and tides as the giant mechanical arm moves back and forth.

Alfred's fascinated with this — that the sea itself lights up the Cathedral, that the changes in the tide are the source of energy, a kind of dynamic plane, and he starts to think about cliffs as a kind of prosthesis of the sea. And he starts to think a lot about his friend, Professor O, who also saw the continuity of movements, networks of temporalities, sequences.

In the following weeks Tiago develops a plan for his new guests. He has them study everything in the Cathedral so they can become messengers, so that they can share the information with other Cathedrals that are just getting started. Trilci and Alice are happy with this mission, but Alfred has a difficult time concentrating. His neurosis gets worse in the cliffs. He's not made for this new world, and he's losing his grip on reality between the voices and hallucinations that take over his mind. Tiago recommends that he write, that writing might be something that can anchor him. But the internal fight between the past, which resists, having lost any fulcrum whatsoever, and the present, which requires of him immediate adaptation, is, for Alfred, long, fierce, overwhelming. In the end, his romantic sensibility of what it is to be a writer, tenacious and irreducible, remains intact with all of his fundamental life values. Only outwardly does he have the will to drown the individual he was and replace him with the external plurality required for the new history.

Then one day, after almost two months in the Cathedral, Alfred finds Tiago at the edge of one of the cliffs and tells him that he's completed his mission, that he's finally finished writing his hallucinations of the world to come, a distant future, half a millennium from now — a world with radiosensing umbrellacycles and angels/troubadours that sing the histories of dead boxers.

Has Alice ever told you about the angel? he asks Tiago. For years she's been telling me about the angel who killed my friend O.

Alfred settles in and, again, tells Tiago about the angel and the Smurfs, that the Smurfs warned him about the dangers of the angel.

And the cat, who knows the story of the angel and the Smurfs all too well, yawns and gets bored looking over the precipice.

Tiago watches the cat while Alfred continues talking, unloading all his narcissistic traumas on a teenager.

The cat persists in his belief that he's exceedingly beautiful. And now Alfred starts to cry as he's talking. And Tiago, impatient, takes a deep breath as the cat looks at him complicitly.

What absolute horse shit! thinks the cat.

And although Tiago doesn't speak Portuguese, he, too, thinks, *What horse shit!* Then he puts his hand on Alfred's back, which Alfred perceives as an act of consolation and thus continues with his self-indulgent, melancholic screed. And so, with all his might, Tiago pushes Alfred over the precipice.

The cat walks to the edge of the cliff and watches his friend in freefall. Then he looks up at Tiago who seems surprised that the cat approves of this murder. Tiago and the cat tell Alice and

Trilcinea that Alfred killed himself after writing the future history of the angel and the Smurfs in the year 2701.

Weeks later, exhausted, but full of new knowledge and experience, Alice and Trilcinea board a ship full of contraband supplies bound for a prison/cathedral in Bolivia for which Tiago has great hopes. And so it is that Trilci and Alice discover one of the disastrous realities of life: sometimes our lovers grow tired of living.

CHAPTER 6:
BACK TO THE YEAR 2017

Wake up, O.

No, let him sleep. Get some rest...

And the voices blur into the distance of his dreams.

Without thinking, he knows.

I'm in the hospital.

More or less awake, he feels beautiful — the after-effect of the mushrooms when the hallucinations stop.

Someone must have rescued me from the den, he thinks. Was it you, Alice?

The doctor and the nurse are talking about him with their backs turned. They have weird hats on.

They say I'm dying. I survived the fall, but when they examined the contusions they discovered that I had cancer. I don't understand why they're talking with their backs to me. They're talking about me as if I weren't listening.

He gathers up every ounce of energy you have to get their attention.

Doctor! he yells almost silently.

The doctor and the nurse turn around. The color of their faces is deep blue, and they're wearing red boxing gloves. With giant, petrified smiles, they tell him he's going to be fine. Everything is just fine.

Author's Note:

Variations of complete paragraphs from the following books were appropriated and creatively modified for this novel:

César Vallejo, "El caso Mayakovski" en *El Arte y la revolución.*

Silvia Rivera-Cusicancqui, en *De chequistas y ovelockas: Una discusión en torno a los talleres textiles.*

Georges Duby. *L'age de cathedrales*

Fred Motten y Stefano Harney. *The University and the Undercommons.*

Amador Fernández Savater, "Doce acciones inspiradoras para burlar la nueva Ley de Seguridad Ciudadana" en *eldiario.es*

Manuel Ramos Otero, "Vivir del cuento" en *Página en blanco y Staccato*

Silvia Federici, *Calibán y la bruja: Mujeres, cuerpo y acumulación originaria.*

Ramón Fernández Durán. *La quiebra del capitalismo global 2000-2030. Preparándonos para el colapso de la Civilización Industrial.*

Jorge Luis Borges, "Nueva refutación del tiempo"

Luis Othoniel Rosa (Puerto Rico, 1985) is the author of the novels *Otra vez me alejo* (Argentina, 2012) and *Caja de fractales* (Argentina/Puerto Rico 2017), and of the study *Comienzos para una estética anarquista: Borges con Macedonio* (Chile, 2016). He studied at the University of Puerto Rico and holds a Ph.D. from Princeton. He teaches Latin American literature at the University of Nebraska. *Down with Gargamel!* is his first book translated into English.